The Cat, The
and Me

By Barwell Hollings

By Barwell Hollings

Table of Contents

The Fortune

The greatest adventure of my life began when the company that employed me, Arbak Gaming, had a successful IPO. My name is Robert Ekans. I'm a computer programmer. I received my master's degree in computer science from UC Santa Cruz. I began working at Arbak Gaming as a summer intern.

But before I go any further, I will tell you a bit about my personal history prior to joining Arbak Gaming. I grew up in a suburb of New York City. When I was young, I was a big fan of medieval stories and movies. I loved books that featured sorcery and magic. As a kid, I'd imagine myself as Merlin the magician from King Arthur's Court. I would put on my wizard's hat and run around with my toy magic wand in hand. I'd cast pretend spells on my stuffed animals and toys. I read Tolkien's Hobbit and Lord of the Rings. Later, I devoured all of the Harry Potter books and movies.

Also, among my favorite movies were the ones about brave knights, castles, and dragons. My hero was Sir Lancelot. That's one reason why I decided to work at Arbak Gaming in the first place. They were working on a medieval sorcery game that included dragons, castles, demons, and brave knights. I was one of the lead programmers on the project. While working on the program, I would imagine what Sir Lancelot and Merlin would do in certain situations. Then, I would add those ideas into the program. I was free to create my own legends featuring the characters that I loved.

Arbak Gaming had recently completed its first round of venture financing and decided to hire me as a full-time employee after my graduation. As an early employee, I was granted a substantial stock option. I also bought more shares during the first round of financing, using money from a trust account that I inherited. Three and a half years later when Arbak Gaming went public, I was allowed to begin selling my stock. A tech stock price bubble was occurring at the time that Arbak Gaming went public. The stock price skyrocketed after the IPO. I began selling my stock near the top of the bubble. The bubble continued for nine months. I continued selling shares during this peak period. This gave me a windfall of almost twenty million dollars. Better yet, since I had bought most of my shares long ago, I was subject to the lower long term capital gain tax rate. I was able to keep most of the profit from the stock sales.

So here I am, a twenty-seven years old with a substantial fortune. I decided to invest the proceeds of the stock sales conservatively rather than rolling it back into the superheated tech stock boom. This turned out to be a prescient decision because the tech stock market bubble burst three months after my last stock sale.

In the ensuing tech stock crash, Arbak Gaming dropped in value by ninety-five percent. Fortunately, I had already sold almost all my Arbak Gaming stock. The conservative investments that I made with the proceeds began returning me a substantial amount of interest and dividends. Enough to sustain myself for the rest of my life.

Prior to selling my Arbak Gaming stock, I had been renting a cheap efficiency apartment in Sunnyvale, California. My lease was up for renewal in three months, so I decided that it was time for me to look for a more permanent residence. I resolved to use some of my stock sale proceeds to purchase rather than rent.

But I did not want to buy just any house. I grew up in New York, in a large Tudor home built in the 1920's. The house felt a bit mysterious and at times spooky to me. Especially the attic and basement. I loved it. I wanted to own a house similar to it if I could find one at a reasonable price. So, I began my search for a large old house with some character. It took two months, but I finally found it.

The Mansion

The house I bought was an old mansion located on just under one acre of land in Mountain View, California. The mansion had two stories of living space, a basement, workshop, and an attic. It was built in the 1920's, well before Mountain View began its transformation from agriculture to a technology center. A faded photograph of the mansion showed that at one time, it was surrounded by orchards. In the mid 1950's the surrounding orchards were turned into a housing development with two- and three-bedroom homes for working class families. Today, Mountain View is the home to thousands of techies working at companies like Facebook, Apple, Google, Microsoft, LinkedIn, and lots of startups. Home prices have been rising rapidly as techies like me come into money from stock sales.

As soon as I set eyes on the mansion, I fell in love with it. Believe me, it needed a lot of work, but that did not deter me from making an offer. The previous owner had passed away and the executors of the estate wanted a quick sale to someone who would take it as is. Fortunately, I had the cash to make a full price offer. I took the mansion as is, with all the furnishings. I will admit that there was quite a bit of junk inside, but that was ok. I had plenty of time to get it cleaned up. You see, I quit my job soon after buying the mansion. I was a free, rich young man, living out my California dream!

There was a bit of mystery about the attic. I only peeked into it once before I bought the mansion. It was dark and there were numerous pieces of furniture covered in old dirty sheets. It reminded me of the attic in my childhood home. I figured that after buying the house, I would have plenty of time to sort through all that stuff, so I left all of it alone until after the sale closed. I wanted the contents of the attic to be a surprise. Like opening a present on Christmas morning!

Initially, I my energy was focused on fixing up the lower two floors and the basement. The basement was quite large. It featured a bar, chairs, and several cabinets. You see, back in prohibition times, this house was the local speakeasy. Locals would come here to drink illegal booze and party. Some of the upstairs rooms served as a brothel. The house carried a bit of notoriety back in the day. From time to time, the speakeasy would be raided and closed by the local police only to be reopened a few weeks later once the heat was off. There was a rumor that a some of the city council members had a silent interest in the speakeasy. Many of the furnishings in the bar area were dated back to that era. I figured that I could host an awesome party in the basement once the mansion was cleaned up.

Oh, I forgot to mention that there is a large, rectangular shaped swimming pool in a courtyard behind the house. It appeared to be in good shape, so that the past owner must have renovated it sometime in the last twenty years or so. I'm a swimmer, so the pool will get some good use. I just need to get it cleaned up and hire a pool service to add chlorine to it on a weekly basis. I'm also considering investing is a solar collector system to heat the pool water. Mountain View gets plenty of sunshine year-round, so why not use it to heat the pool! It certainly would save on the heating bill and extend the number of months that I can use it.

It's my first day in my mansion. With my iPhone in hand, I take pictures of everything on the first two floors. The kitchen is quite dated. The cabinets are faded, and the counter cracked. I make a note that this is an area where I will be applying my amateur carpentry and re-finishing skills. The stove is out of date, but quaint looking. I will keep it if it works. The refrigerator and dish washer were recently updated. I'll keep them for sure. There is a small guest bedroom and bath on this floor, perhaps it was a maid quarters at one time. The hallway has another bathroom. The bathroom has been updated recently as well.

I gradually make my way up to the second floor. Here there are three bedrooms and a study. The master bedroom is large and has an adjoining bathroom with an updated walk-in shower. The other two bedrooms share a large adjoining common bathroom. There is one more small bathroom in the hallway. All the bathrooms could use some updating, but the plumbing fixtures work just fine. Renovating the bathrooms will be a multiyear project for sure.

Next, I decide to take the winding stairway up to the attic. At the top of the stairs, there is a small landing and a screen door that leads directly into the attic storage area. I open the door and step inside. I'm surrounded by a variety of items. Most are covered with old dust covered sheets. I'm guessing that some of the items have been covered for decades, maybe more!

I pull the sheet off each item to reveal what is underneath. One item is a very old baby carriage. Its literally a basinet on wheels with a half hood covering where the baby's head would lie. Next to it is an old crib and diaper changing table. They look like they were from the 1950's. Leaning against the wall are two large paintings. The frames are cracked. I wonder if the paintings carry any value. I will have to bring them downstairs and take a closer look later. If I can read the artist's name, I can search for it on the internet. If the artists are known, I will have an appraiser value them.

I find an old hand operated sewing machine sitting on a table. Next to it is a vintage mechanical typewriter. Both appear to be in poor shape but could be cleaned and restored if they carry some antique value. Various other items are scattered about the floor. Some are old toys and dolls. They look pretty beat up.

Finally, I uncover an object leaning against the far wall. It's a bedframe set. The headboard and footboard are a vintage wrought iron. There are also a set of side rails to which the headboard and footboard can be mounted. I pull the set into the center of the room to get a better look at it. I lay the pieces out on the floor. They all appear to fit together. The set looks very old but sturdy. I'm betting that the headboard and footboard pre-date the mansion by a lot. I also wonder why this bed is up in the attic when It's so much more elegant than the bedframe sets that I have found in the bedrooms. On closer inspection, I notice that the headboard and footboard each have a strange looking gemstone embedded in the center of an even stranger circular design. Each gemstone appears to be reddish in color. They're old, scratched and faded. My first impression is that they must have been intended for ornamental purposes. They likely have little value except as part of the frame set. Nevertheless, I really like them.

I'm thinking that I will move this frame set down to the master bedroom and use it to sleep on. I will have to find a suitable mattress and box spring to fit on the frame. I doubt that this is a standard size that I can buy from a local mattress store.

It's getting late, and I'm hungry. I decide that I will come back up to the attic tomorrow, move the bedframe set downstairs and assemble it. So, I descend the staircases to the first floor and enter the kitchen. I'm going to test out the stove by cooking up some hamburgers. I will also steam some vegetables in a pot. Later, I relax in front of the TV. Yes! I'm sitting in my own mansion. I'm thinking about giving it a suitable name. Maybe Chateau Ekans!

The Bedframe

It's the following morning. I get up and take a walk around the grounds of my property. There is a stone wall separating one side of the property from the street. I find a door in the stone wall. Along the back of the property, and the other side, there is a tall wooden fence. Both border a park and elementary school yard.

The front of the house is set back from the street. The front yard is a bit overgrown with weeds. There are two garden beds, some bushes and two large trees. The yard will need some work. I resolve that I will hire a gardener to stop by every two weeks and trim things up.

All in all, I think that I got a pretty good deal with my purchase of Chateau Ekans! So, I go back inside and make a cup of tea. I eat breakfast and spend the rest of the morning reorganizing the inside of the house to make it livable. In the afternoon, I return to the attic and carry the bedframe pieces downstairs to the bedroom. There, I put it back together again and take some measurements. I go online to see if any standard mattress sets will fit the bed. If none are available, I will have to order a custom mattress set.

Sure enough, It's not a standard size. I find a company online that deals in custom mattress sizes. I speak with the owner and give her my requirements. Surprisingly, she has a set available in her warehouse. It was for an order that got cancelled. She comments, "You must have a very old frame. Many of my customers have old frames. This size dates back almost three hundred years. Maybe more!"

I'm blown away. Could it be that this frame set is that old? Or is it a reproduction? No matter, I like the frame, and I will sleep on this bed once I have the mattress and box spring. Until then, I'm sleeping on a bed in one of the smaller bedrooms.

The mattress and box spring are delivered five days later. The delivery people unwrap them and place them on my bed frame. It fits perfectly. When the delivery people leave, I lie down on the bed to see how it feels. It's quite comfortable. Then I notice something strange happening. I could swear that the red gemstone on the footboard suddenly glowed. I continue to stare at it, but the glowing does not repeat. I guess that maybe the sunlight through the window hit it briefly at the right angle to cause the glowing effect. Then the sun moved out of position. Or maybe It was just my overactive imagination!

I get my pillows, sheets and blanket and fit them onto the bed. I'm ready for the first night's sleep on the bed. It's eleven o'clock in the evening, and I'm getting tired. So, I change into my pajamas, wash up and crawl into bed. At first it feels strange to be sleeping in this new room, but in moments I'm fast asleep.

That night, I dream that I'm rowing a boat across a lake, or maybe it's a slow flowing river. I'm surrounded by a fog, but I keep rowing. I have a sense that something lies just ahead of me. The fog lifts just enough that I can see a structure of some kind. I continue rowing towards the structure. The structure is becoming clearer now. It looks like a large white medieval castle. As I get closer, the walls of the castle tower over me. I reach the shore on one side of the castle. After stepping off the boat, I pull it onto the shore and place the oars inside it. I walk up to the wall and feel the stones. They're cold to the touch. I look up. The walls must be at least twenty feet high. The stones that make up the castle walls appear to be pure white in color. I find this odd because I thought that most castles are very old and dark unless they were recently whitewashed or plastered white.

So, I begin walking along the outside perimeter of the wall until I reach a large gate. The door to the gate is made of two large wooden pieces that meet in the middle. All along the walls I see banners rising. The banners depict an image of either a dragon or a panther.

I want to see what is inside this white castle, but the gate is closed. I call out for someone to open it, but no one responds. So, I continue to walk around the wall looking for another gate or door, but none is to be found. It's then that I hear a distinct sound. It’s not a normal human sound. I listen more closely. I hear it again, but more clearly this time, “Meow. Meow.” I think, *could that be coming from a cat? What is a cat doing here at this castle?* I begin searching around the outside wall for the cat. Each time the cat meows, I get a little closer, but I just can’t locate it.

I suddenly wake up. I’m in my master bedroom, staring up at the ceiling. I think, *that was a strange dream!* An empty castle and a phantom cat! For the next few minutes, I reflect on my dream. I look at the antique footboard, with the red gemstone embedded in it. I wonder if somehow this bedframe influenced my dream! Or maybe it's my imagination again. I climb out of bed and change into my clothes. I have a lot of work to do today. I better get started soon.

The next evening, I have a similar dream, but this time I'm roaming around inside the white castle! I have no idea how I got in there. I call out, "Is anyone here?" Again, no one replies to my call. I continue exploring the inside of the castle. Everything looks so authentic. I think about scenes from medieval movies that I have watched. The set is all laid out before me except there are no actors. Could this be some sort of movie set? I find a stall where a blacksmith would be working metals. The stall contains numerous tables and a forge. The forge is smoldering, an indication that there was recent activity here. The tables and other fixtures in the stall appear to be rather low to the ground implying that this blacksmith was rather short in stature. I see a sword and several daggers sitting on a table. I pick one up. It has texture and fine detail. The blade looks sharp. I see a shield leaning up against the wall. I take a close look at it. It has the same dragon depiction that I saw on some of the banners mounted on the castle walls. Yet another shield depicts a panther.

I find other stalls with a variety of goods on display. Some have vegetables, others display textiles and clothing, yet not a person is around. I pick up a small rug. It has an engraved depiction of a person with pointed ears tilling the ground with a hoe. Another textile depicts a dwarfish looking family gathered around a table eating. The table has bowls filled with fruits and vegetables. I realize that these textile designs reflect scenes from daily life, but with elves and dwarfs, instead of humans! Someone must have woven all of these textiles. But where are they?

Suddenly I hear a cat meowing. Once again, I search for the cat but cannot find it despite the meow sounds getting closer. A moment later, I wake up in my bedroom. I wonder why I have had this same dream on two consecutive nights.

Over the following nights, I have similar dreams. The castle is exactly the same in every detail and the cat always meows but remains out of sight. Very strange! In one dream, I see an object flying high up in the sky. It's too far away to clearly identify it. Perhaps it's a large bird? But birds don't typically fly so high. This object has an enormous wingspan and long thin tail. I wonder what kind of bird has those characteristics? The largest known bird is the wandering albatross. But does not have a long tail.

After each dream, I wake up in my bed staring at the red gemstone embedded in the footboard. *Did I just see it glow again? Are my eyes playing tricks on me?* I'm wondering, what's up with the red gemstone anyway? Could it have some sort of mystical power?

Grimalkin

It's Saturday afternoon. I have just finished painting one of the small bedrooms. I'm thirsty so I go down to the kitchen to get a bottle of water from the refrigerator. When I return to the small bedroom to put away the paint, drop cloths and brushes, I hear a soft scurrying sound coming from the hardwood floor in the hallway. I hope that's not a critter running around inside my house. Roof rats are a common pest in this area. Squirrels have also been known to creep into a house and take up residency.

I step into the hallway just in time to see a bushy black tail disappear into the master bedroom. I quietly walk down the hallway and into the master bedroom. I step into the doorway and look over at my bed. Casually lying on the bed with one leg draped over the side is the largest black cats that I have ever seen. I just stand there watching it. I notice that the cat has a gold chain around its neck with a pendent hanging from it. It's a beautiful cat with long black hair and penetrating green eyes.

The cat is studying me with a rather inquisitive expression. It does not budge. It appears very comfortable where it is. I ask, "What are you doing here my furry friend?" The cat responds with a meow. It still does not budge. The meow sound immediately reminds me of the phantom meowing cat from my dreams.

I slowly approach the cat. I can see the pendant more clearly now. It's a beautiful piece of gold jewelry and it fits perfectly on the cat. In the center of the pendent is a small reddish stone similar to the ones on my bedposts. The red stone has a bright almost sparkling. What is a cat doing with a piece of fine jewelry around its neck? I'm thinking that whoever owns this cat must be rich.

The cat tracks my every move with its eyes. I'm standing in front of the cat. I reach down and gently stroke its head. The cat looks up at me and begins to purr. I sit down on the bed next to the cat. It keeps gazing into my eyes while I stroke it. This is the most beautiful cat that I have ever seen. It looks very well cared for.

I look at the collar more closely. The red gem is a smaller version of the stones embedded in the headboard and footboard of my bed. Only this stone is not worn at all. Then I notice a flat section on the chain. I take a closer look at it expecting to find the cat owner's name. Instead, I see one word inscribed,

Grimalkin. That name is familiar to me. I love fantasy stories. I recall that the name Grimalkin, is attributed to cats involved in witchcraft and sorcery tales. It also is attributed to feline faeries. I have never known a modern-day cat to carry this name. Its owner must be into medieval magic and witchcraft.

Grimalkin and I are sitting there gazing at each other. It's like we're communicating in some higher level. Then Grimalkin gets up on all fours and hops off the bed. It stands there briefly and stretches. Then Grimalkin walks underneath the bed. I get off the bed and peer under it expecting to see Grimalkin hiding there, but there is nothing to see. The cat is gone! I look around the room to see if maybe it snuck away without me noticing. The windows are closed as is the closet door. Only the door to the bedroom is open. I get up and look down the hallway. Then I search the other bedrooms and bathrooms. Grimalkin is nowhere to be found. The cat has just vanished!

Maybe this is a very clever cat? I check the surveillance cameras that I have installed around the house thinking that Grimalkin should show up on one of them. No luck there either. The camera footage shows my movements but does not reveal the cat either coming or going. Very strange indeed!

Anyway, I clean up the paint in the small bedroom and go out to get a bite to eat at a local fast-food restaurant. When I get home, I do internet searches on the name, Grimalkin. Sure enough, this confirms my earlier suspicions about the origins of the name. It's associated with witches, magic, and sorcery. Grimalkin appears in numerous fantasy tales as well.

Have I stumbled upon a medieval riddle of some sort? After all, the clues are before me:

A cat named Grimalkin with a pendent around its neck.

A bed frame set embedded with strange glowing red gemstones matching the gemstone on Grimalkin's pendent.

Strange dreams about a pure white castle with a phantom cat meowing at me. Could that be Grimalkin?

A large mysterious object flying high up in the sky.

Anyway, I'm tired and it's time for bed. I lie down on my mattress. My head is filled with thoughts about Grimalkin, the white castle, and the red gemstones. Soon I fall asleep and begin dreaming.

The Throne Room

In my dream, I'm back in the same boat on the lake. I'm rowing towards the same pure white castle. This time there is no fog on the lake. I can see everything clearly. I look up at the sky and see not one, but five of the huge flying creatures circling high over the castle.

Once again, I pull the boat ashore, stow the oars and walk up to the castle wall. After walking around the perimeter of the wall, I reach the main gate. This time, the main gate opens I stand there for a moment and look up at the walls. I can see the dragon and panther banners are still mounted exactly where they were in my previous dreams. I take a breath and walk through the gate. Once again, there is no one present inside the castle.

I walk into the main courtyard and notice an open door in the side of a large structure. This structure appears to be in the center of the castle. I look up and see that there is a tall tower above it. I walk through the open door and into a long hallway. I hear sounds coming from the far end of the hallway. I decide to follow the sounds to investigate its source. At the end of the hallway, I find another open doorway. I step inside. What I see is absolutely mind blowing. At my feet is a long, narrow red carpet perhaps fifty feet long. It's leading towards an object that look like a golden throne chair with a red cushion on its seat. On either side of the carpet are dozens of cats of various sizes. All are adorned with fancy collars or chains around their necks. Most of the cats are solid black or dark gray in color but there are a few with mixed coats. Each cats' head is turned towards the throne. They appear to be listening intently.

I begin walking down the carpet towards the throne. As I get closer, I cannot believe what I'm seeing. Casually relaxing on the throne chair is a large, beautiful black longhair cat. I immediately recognize the pendant around the cat's neck. It's Grimalkin, the cat that visited me in my mansion!

Our eyes meet. Then, I sense a voice inside my head saying, "Welcome to the White Castle, Robert!" I'm thinking, "How's this possible?" I respond by asking, "Grimalkin, what am I doing here? What is this place? And who are you, really? Is this a dream that I'm having? What were you doing in my mansion the other day?"

Grimalkin replies, “Robert, I will answer your questions in good time. But for now, I’m happy that you have joined us.” I notice that all the cats have turned towards me. Many are softly meowing to each other. I get the impression that they must be commenting about me to each other using their cat language. Grimalkin issues a series of meows. Then, one by one each cat walks up to me. I stroke each one gently as they pass in front of me. Some purr. Others meow and blink their eyes. I take these as positive reactions. When all the cats have returned to their original positions, Grimalkin meows to them. One by one the cats take turns meowing back. This reminds me of a voice count conducted in a meeting. Are these cats following a form of parliamentary procedure? If so, wonder if they are replying, “Yea.” Or “Nay”?

After the last cat has responded, Grimalkin meows several times. Her voice speaks to me inside my head once more. She says, “Robert, my fellow feline wizards, and witches have agreed that they like you. You will be allowed to visit our home here in the White Castle any time you wish. Of course, for now, that will only be possible in your dreams! While sleeping in the bed with the red gemstones.”

I'm utterly confused now. I respond by asking, "Witches? Wizards? Dreams?" Grimalkin answers, "Robert, I will answer all your questions. But first, why don't you take a seat?" I look around behind me for a chair to sit on, but there is none to be found. I turn back towards Grimalkin and there in front of me is a chair. I ask, "Where did that come from? It was not there a minute ago." Grimalkin responds, "Robert, you are forgetting where you are. You are in a very special place. Objects and even entities materialize and disappear here all the time!"

I walk over to the chair and sit down. Then I smile at Grimalkin and say, "I'm ready." Grimalkin gives me a sly cat grin and begins to fill up my mind with thoughts. She asks, "What would you like to know first?"

I reply, "Am I dreaming?"

"You most certainly are."

"So, none of this is real?"

"In a way, yes. But also, no."

"What do you mean by that answer?"

"You are dreaming, but the White Castle does exist. The White Castle is part of your dream because that's the only way you can be here right now. But for the rest of us cats, the White Castle very real. You see, we're not ordinary cats. We're an ancient species with telepathic powers, among other things. We're the preferred companions of witches, wizards, and sorcerers because of our special abilities. Most humans could never understand entities that possess paranormal abilities. They tend to react with fear and sometimes violence as evidenced by the witch burnings and hangings that blot human history. On the other hand, we cats are a lot more flexible in our thinking."

"Then why am I here? Am I not a typical human? I'm certainly not a cat! "

"Robert, you are here because you too are special. You don't think as typical humans do. You are also here because of the bedframe. That's how I found you in the first place."

Grimalkin goes on to tell the story of the bedframe. It was the possession of her witch mistress and teacher, a witch named Glynda. Glynda lived in a cottage hidden in the woods in medieval England. She raised Grimalkin from a kitten. Glynda loved Grimalkin and passed on to her many of her special powers of witchcraft and magic. But Glynda grew old. Before passing on, she decided to pass on one more gift. This was the most powerful gift of her life. The wrought iron bed that Glynda slept on was no ordinary bed. It was an enchanted medium used as a portal for transference between the human world and the world of the White Castle. It was used by Glynda to transport herself to other places as well. Glynda taught Grimalkin the secrets of the red gemstones embedded in the headboard and footboard of the bedframe. Most important, she taught Grimalkin how to cast a spell such that the portal powers of the red gemstones can be activated and manipulated as a portal. Glynda also gave Grimalkin the pendant that she's wearing around her neck.

Grimalkin sat by Glynda's side until she passed away. She was very sad, but also hopeful for the future and grateful for the gifts that Glynda had bequeathed to her. Once in possession of the bed, Grimalkin began using it as a portal to travel back and forth between the world of humans and the White Castle. At the White Castle, she learned that many of the secrets of deceased witches, wizards and sorcerers had been passed on to their beloved cats. The cats congregated together in the White

Castle. But during one of Grimalkin's trips to the White Castle, Glynda's cottage was discovered by a group of humans who were seeking to root out the witches who lived in the English countryside. They found Glynda's bed and disassembled it. They had no idea about its powers. The bed was hidden away in a dungeon. For nearly three hundred years, the bed was left there and forgotten. Its portal powers were no longer accessible to Grimalkin.

Then one day, a wealthy antique collector bought the furnishings of a medieval English castle. Inside the dungeon, he found the bed frame. He packed it up and brought it to the new world, but instead of reassembling it, he stored it in the attic of his mansion and forgot about it. It stayed there for several generations until Robert, found it. When Robert carefully reconstructed the bed, he also reactivated its special portal power. Grimalkin explains that the red gemstones embedded in the headboard and footboard only have special powers when spaced apart the correct distance. They then activate a portal between the world of humans and the world of the White Castle.

Grimalkin says, "I immediately sensed that the portal was active once more. That's when I decided to pay you a visit. I must say that it was refreshing to be able to easily move between the White Castle and the world of humans again! I must also comment that things have certainly changed in the human world. When I peered out your window, I saw great machines moving about on the road in front of your home. They moved without the use of horses or mules. It appeared magical to me."

I'm stunned by what Grimalkin has told me. I'm wondering how I found myself in the middle of this tale of magical medieval drama. I ask, "So why did you bring me here to the White Castle?"

Grimalkin replies, "I sensed in you many promising traits. You are open minded to all possibilities. You have interests in magic and sorcery. And hidden within you is a yet untapped power. I suspect you may have distant relatives who had special powers as well. Perhaps some of those abilities were passed on to you."

I know that my family were among the first to arrive in the new world from England. I recall stories about my ancestors. There is one tale about a relative who was accused of witchcraft and burned at the stake in the 1690's. That was towards the end of the Salem Witch Trials. Could it be that the old family stories are true?

Grimalkin says, “I can help you to unlock the powers that reside inside you. And in return,

you can introduce me to this fascinating world that you live in. It’s so different from medieval England.”

This is a lot for me to digest. I also have a nagging suspicion that this is just one hell of a dream that I’m experiencing. I reply, “Grimalkin, I will have to sleep on this.” Grimalkin replies, “Robert, you are sleeping!” Then she says, “I understand. I will give you some time to think about what I have said. You can go back to your home now!”

It seems like a moment later, I’m lying in my bed staring at the ceiling. I’m thinking that this was one heck of a dream! It was so vivid. The cats, Grimalkin, the White Castle, and throne room! I had never dreamed in such precision detail before. I can also recall every telepathic thought that I received from Grimalkin.

So, I get up and look out the window. I see the back yard, the pool, and a lot of overgrown vegetation. Yes, I’m definitely back home in Mountain View! So, I go downstairs and get some food. I have a lot of work planned for today. I’m going to paint another bedroom and then work in the back yard. Later I will take a swim in the pool. The water is a bit cold because I have not yet installed the solar collector heating system. That's scheduled for next week. The system should raise the water temperature a good five to ten degrees. That will extend the usefulness of the pool to almost nine months of the year. I'm considering purchasing an automated pool cover as well.

The bedroom that I'm painting is smaller than the master. It takes about half the time to paint. I'm done by eleven thirty in the morning. So, I fix myself a sandwich for lunch. Then I set out to start the cleanup of the back yard. It's overgrown with weeds and there are all kinds of objects hiding under the tall grass and weeds. The work is hard. I pull up a portable compost bin and fill it up with the weeds and other vegetation. After two hours the bin is full, and I've done enough of weed pulling. I'm ready for that swim!

I go back inside the house and put on my swimsuit and grab a towel. I enter the pool slowly. The water is a bit cool, but tolerable. I'm happy that I've decided to invest in that solar collector system.

I start off with ten laps of breaststroke and then switch to freestyle. I was on the swim team in high school and swam occasionally in college. Swimming has always been one of my favorite exercises because it gives me a full body workout. I'm usually relaxed when my workout is done. While swimming I can do a lot of thinking. My mind begins to drift to the crazy dreams that I have been having.

When I swim freestyle, I alternate my breathing from side to side. I can occasionally catch a glimpse of the sides of the pool when I take a breath. On my twentieth lap, I notice a dark colored critter sitting next to the side of the pool. I'm thinking it could be a squirrel or worse yet, a rat! When, I reach the far side of the pool, I stop and turn to see what the thing is. Well, it's not a squirrel or rat! Sitting quietly watching me is a large black cat with a pendant around in's neck. I call out, "Grimalkin, is that you?" The reply comes inside my head, "Who else did you think it could be? But please don't let me disturb your swim. You are quite good I must say. I've never seen a human that could swim so smoothly as you!"

I ask, "What are you doing here?" Grimalkin replies, "Just visiting! I must admit, you have a nice place. Very classy compared to the small houses nearby. Are you the only human living here? Do you have servant? Or a girlfriend, mistress or wife?"

I reply, “Grimalkin, it’s just me here. I’m not married, and I don’t have a girlfriend right now. I’m too busy fixing up this house. Why do you ask?”

Grimalkin replies. “Well, I know someone in a similar situation as you. She’s not seeing anyone right now. Her name is Emilia. She’s quite beautiful and intelligent. I’m sure that you will like her.” I reply, “So now you are playing matchmaker? How do you know Emilia anyway? All your companions in the White Castle are cats. I did not see any humans among them. Are you trying to fix me up with a cat?”

Grimalkin replies, “Robert, of course not. I have been able to read your thoughts. I’m certain that Emilia would be a good match for you. You see, you have only scratched the surface of the entities who frequent the White Castle and the environs around it. Emilia is very special. She comes and visits us almost every day. She’s a very dear friend.

Grimalkin flashes an image of beautiful young woman into my mind. After seeing the image, I must admit his offer to introduce us is enticing. Then I suddenly snap back to reality. I ask, “Grimalkin, what are you really doing here? I’m sure it’s not only to play fantasy matchmaker!”

Grimalkin replies, “Robert, you will soon find out all the details, but It’s too complicated a story to tell in one sitting. Besides, I know that you are looking for a unique adventure. My world can offer that to you.”

Grimalkin continues, “For my part, I want to learn more about your world. I was hoping you could show me around sometime.”

I reply, “I’d love to show you around, but I can’t take a cat with me just anywhere. No offence, but animals are not allowed in some places. They would see you and turn me away. Also, most dogs would go crazy at the first sight of a cat.” Grimalkin replies, “They can’t turn you away if they don’t see me. I can handle the dogs as well.”

“Are you asking me to hide you?”

“No, Robert. You can see me, but they can’t”

“You’re saying that only I can see you?”

“Robert, you can always see and hear me. It’s one of your powers. The power of imagination is strong in you. But for others, they can see me only if I choose for them to do so."

I think about this a moment, then I ask, "Are you saying you're my imaginary friend?"

Grimalkin replies, "In a manner of speaking, yes. But rest assured, I'm very real as you will discover."

Then Grimalkin says, "Enough talking, I feel like a swim." Grimalkin launches herself into the pool. She bobs up and begins swimming with all fours across the pool.

I say, "I thought that cats hated water?" Grimalkin replies, "Not this cat! The water looked so inviting that I just had to jump in!" I resume my swimming using a breaststroke so that I can watch Grimalkin. I'm actually lap swimming with Grimalkin!

After a few more laps, Grimalkin swims over to the steps and climbs out of the pool. There she shakes herself off and comments, "That was quite refreshing. Back at the White Castle, I occasionally take a swim in the lake, but I must be careful to avoid being spotted by the serpents who hide just under the surface of the water. They can be vicious. It's safer to swim when Emilia is around. The serpents know better than to get too close when she's present."

I'm curious to meet Emilia now. A beautiful woman who can scare away sea serpents. This story is getting crazier by the minute!

Grimalkin then says, "I need to get back to the White Castle now. I'll see you in your dream tonight. Hopefully I can introduce you to Emilia then." Having said that, Grimalkin walks back into the house. I'm sure that she's scurrying up the steps and under the bed in the master bedroom. I'm left standing in the pool wondering if all this has really happened, or if I've lost my mind! I pick up my towel and dry off. Then I go upstairs and take a hot shower, dress, and prepare dinner. I realize that I can't wait to fall asleep tonight. I want to meet Grimalkin's friend Emilia!

Emilia

It's getting late so I enter the main bedroom and lie down on the bed. I'm wondering if my dreams will take me back to the White Castle again. Will I be greeted by Grimalkin? Will I be introduced to Emilia? The swim has relaxed me. In moments, I'm fast asleep.

I find myself standing in a field near the outer wall of the White Castle. I look over at it. I can see the main gate, high walls and a towers rising inside. The sky is mostly clear and there are a few high clouds. It's a beautiful day. I don't see anyone around me, so I begin to walk towards the White Castle. Then I hear a voice inside my head saying, "Robert, where are you going? I thought you wanted to meet Emilia?"

I turn around and see Grimalkin standing in the grass. I reply, "Grimalkin, I was looking around for you. Now here you are!"

Grimalkin replies, "If we wait here a few minutes, I'm sure that Emilia will spot us and come over. She has excellent vision you know!"

So, I keep looking out at the field to see if someone is approaching. I also look over to the gate of the White Castle. I say, "I don't see anyone around us."

Grimalkin says, "Robert, you are looking in the wrong places." Grimalkin looks up towards the sky. I do too. That's when I see an object approaching from above us. As it gets closer, I can see that the object has a long body attached to two massive wings. The object also has a long tail trailing behind it. It's too large to be a hawk, eagle of albatross.

Now it's close enough That I can see its head. It has a reptilian look about it. Suddenly, I know what the object is. This thought takes my breath away. I turn towards Grimalkin and ask, "Is Emilia a dragon?" Grimalkin lets out a meow. I take that as a yes!

In another moment, the dragon sets foot on the field not twenty feet from where I'm standing. It's huge, with two bright green eyes, a long muzzle with two rows of long sharp teeth. At the end of each wing is a claw like hand. The dragon lets out a terrifying roar and then walks forward towards us. I can feel it's hot breath. It's a beautiful yet frightening creature, right out of a fairy tale. Grimalkin says, "Robert, this is my friend, Emilia!" The dragon begins speaking. It says, "Robert, I'm Emilia, I'm very pleased to meet you. Grimalkin has told me about you. He said that you live in a beautiful mansion in the human world. Grimalkin also said that you are very nice and have a lot of potential."

I reply, "Emilia, Grimalkin told me about you too, but he did not mention that you were in fact, a dragon." At that, Emilia says, "Oh, I see, you were not expecting to meet a dragon, were you?" The she says. "Maybe this will help to clarify things!"

Emilia's dragon body begins to glow, undulate, and then shrink in size. A moment later I can see a human body materialize. I'm amazed at the transformation that I'm witnessing. A tall, beautiful woman is standing where the huge fairytale dragon once stood. She's dressed as a medieval warrior queen. There is a tiara on her head and a longsword sheathed to a belt around her waist. Emilia is wearing white chain mail armor with the insignia of a dragon on the front. The armor almost glows. It has an aura of enchantment about it.

Emilia has shoulder length auburn hair, bright green eyes, and light brown skin tone. She has the athletic build of an athlete. Emilia is stunning! I'm standing there with my jaw hanging open. I'm unable to speak. The next thing I hear is Grimalkin sniping, "What's the matter Robert? Cat got your tongue?"

I ask Emilia, "How? How did you do that? One moment you're a fearsome dragon and the next you are a beautiful warrior queen!" Emilia laughs and replies, "Robert, you must remember where you are. This is not the world of humans. Here things here are a bit different than were you come from!"

I reply, "You bet they're different! In the human world, my job was to create fantasy characters and enchanted worlds inside of video games. But this is no video game. Or is it?" Emilia asks, "Robert, what exactly is a video game?" I begin to chuckle. I respond, "Emilia, I will explain that in due time. For now, I'm absolutely thrilled to meet you!" This elicits a big smile from Emilia, she replies, "Robert, I'm thrilled to meet you too!"

Grimalkin says, "Let's go back to the White Castle and have a chat."

The Throne Room

While we're walking over to the White Castle, Emilia keeps looking over at me and smiling. I smile back. I must admit, meeting Emilia has been exciting. I really don't care if this is just a dream or a bout of insanity. I don't want it to end. I receive a thought from Grimalkin, "Robert, I was right about Emilia. I can sense that you like her. She likes you too!" I see no need to reply to this question because the answer is obvious.

The castle doors open, and we enter. A few minutes later we're in the throne room. As we walk down the red carpet, I view three fancy chairs facing each other in a triangle. Emilia and I each sit down in a chair. Grimalkin jumps up on the padded cushion of the third chair and relaxes. When I look over at Emilia, I see that her chain mail armor and sword are gone. In its place is a tight-fitting fine leather outfit with a plunging neckline. It's a very provocative look. I can't help but think that it's for my benefit. Among her various abilities, Emilia is a quick-change artist! Or maybe it's just how things happen in this magical world.

Grimalkin begins by saying, “Robert, Emilia also has telepathic abilities. I can speak to both of you telepathically and you can respond verbally. I take note of this. I also wonder how easily Emilia can read my thoughts. She likely is aware of the effect that her presence is having on me.

I begin by asking Emilia about her ability to transform into a dragon. She tells me that she was born with this ability. She can change into a dragon anytime she wants. It comes in handy when she needs to cover long distances in a short period of time. She also likes to view her world from up in the sky. Additionally, her dragon body comes in handy when confronting a powerful adversary.

I ask Emilia if she can breathe fire when in her dragon body. She replies that she can but must be careful to conserve that ability because her dragon body is limited in how many fiery exhalations she can make before being temporarily tapped out. She’ll then have to wait until the fire emitting glands in her throat of her dragon body are recharged. I find this interesting. Even in this fantasy land, there are physical limitations.

Then I ask Emilia how old she is. What were her earliest recollections? She replies, “I really cannot say when I was born. It was so long ago. I will tell you that I have visited the human world many times in the past. I have even lived there and loved there."

I ask, "Loved? You loved humans in the past?" Emilia replies, "Yes, there have been several. My first human love was a dashing Viking named Ragnar. He and I went into many battles together. Back then I was known to the Vikings as Lagertha, queen of the shield maidens. But I eventually became disillusioned by the Vikings ruthless ways. I don't approve of raiding and slaughtering innocents. So, Ragnar and I parted ways. But Ragnar was only the first of many human loves that would follow. I was particularly fond of a brave knight named Sir Lancelot. Perhaps you have heard of him?"

I'm shocked by her answer. I say, "Sir Lancelot? He was one of my childhood heroes. I would read fables of his exploits. But I did not know that he was an actual real person! I thought that he was just a legend. What happened between you and Lancelot?"

Emilia replies, "Robert, Sir Lancelot was very real indeed. He and I spent many good years together, but he eventually fell in love with Queen

Guinevere. I advised him that this was a dangerous relationship, but he did not listen. I decided it was time to leave and find new adventures.

There were a few others after Lancelot. Most were less famous. Each time I found a new love, some would eventually grow old and die. Others died in battle. You see, humans are vulnerable and have such short lifespans. On the other hand, I have lived a very long time, yet have barely aged. But I will always remember Sir Lancelot. He and I enjoyed the time we had together. He was a brave and dashing knight. Often, we would go into battle together against the enemies of the kingdom. Sometimes I would don my armor and fight as a human. Other times, when the odds we greatly stacked against us, I would revert to my dragon body and smite our enemies with my fiery breath. Always we prevailed!"

I respond, "But some of the stories about Lancelot describe him fighting a dragon. Were you the dragon he fought?" Emilia laughs and replies, "Sir Lancelot and I were always fooling the peasants and townspeople. In one village, the townspeople claimed that an evil monster was threatening them and eating their sheep. We knew that this was the product of their imaginations. So, Sir Lancelot and I play acted in a fight where he slayed me. I collapsed and then vanished into thin air. This seemed to appease the villagers. But over time the story changed. Villagers have such vivid imaginations. That's another reason why I tried not to change form into a dragon in front of humans. They would make up crazy stories about me."

"But the biggest problem for me or any other dragon was the human kings with daughters. You see, wherever I traveled in the human world, there was always a king who would offer the hand of his daughter to the bravest knight in the kingdom. To prove his bravery, the knight would have to slay a dragon and bring its severed head before the king. Such a waste! Not all dragons can change form as easily as I, so they were forced to fight when cornered by a knight. Many a brave knight ended up incinerated by a dragons' fiery breath."

I'm beginning to wonder if all the stories that Emilia is telling me are true. I don't doubt that she's an actual dragon. I saw that with my own eyes. But the stories about Ragnar and Lancelot seem a bit farfetched. Or are they? Did she pluck these characters from my mind? Or are the stories real? Maybe Emilia is trying to impress me for some reason?"

I also realize that I'm flirting with an immortal being, yet I'm a human with limited abilities and a short lifespan. Emilia looks at me. She says, "Robert, I can read your emotions and thoughts. You have been brought to this magical land as a mortal human, and you are concerned about why you are here. All I can say is that you should put these concerns aside because there is more to you than you realize. That's why Grimalkin has brought you here. You are more like us than you could possibly imagine!"

Grimalkin asks, "Robert, do you want to tap into your inner power? If so, we can help you do that. You are a special human. Even more so than Ragnar, Sir Lancelot, and a host of others. We have never brought a human here except for you and one other.

I ask, "Who was that?"

"Merlin."

"Merlin the magician from King Arthur's Court? Really?"

"Yes, Merlin. But he's very old now. He lives up in the main tower of the White Castle. Occasionally, he comes down to the throne room and sits by the throne. It reminds him of the old times back in King Arthur's Court. Merlin has never been quite the same since then! I keep telling him to move on from the glories of the past, but Merlin is stubborn. He replies that things now are just not the same as back then! But Merlin has many magical powers and a trove of knowledge. We frequently consult with him when a problem arises that we cannot solve. Sometimes he cooperates but other times he tells us to go away. Like I said, Merlin is very stubborn!"

I reply, "Will I be able to meet Merlin?" Grimalkin replies, "You will meet Merlin when he decides to meet you."

Emilia asks me about my life. I reply that I was born in a place called New York. Then my family moved to the suburbs. I lived there until the age of seventeen. When in high school, I was good at mathematics and science. After graduation, I went to college to study computer science. Emilia asks, "Is that where you became interested in magic and medieval history? And what is computer science?"

I reply, "I was interested in magic much earlier than that. I also read about Ragnar, Lagartha, and the Vikings. Also, Sir Lancelot and King Arthur's court. In addition to that, I read a lot of Greek, Roman, Norse, and Chinese mythology. There are many dragons and monsters described in those stories and myths."

Emilia replies, "I hope you don't think that I'm a monster?" I quickly reply, "Oh, of course not! You are very nice. I could never think of you as a monster! It's just that humans tend to be afraid of things that they don't understand. Their fears emerge in stories of brave heroes facing evil monsters." Emilia smiles and says, "Thank you for clarifying that."

I continue to describe how in college, I joined the medieval history club. We studied the customs of the people of that time. Some of us came to meetings dressed as knights. We would also hold mock sword fights using blunted swords. I even learned to ride a horse and participated in a few jousts. I usually ended up being knocked off my horse by my opponent.

Emilia says, "That's most impressive. I would like to test your sword fighting skills. Perhaps we can do some training together later." I reply, "Emilia, I would love to, but I must admit that I'm not very good at sword fighting." Emilia replies, "You probably did not have a good teacher." Grimalkin adds, "Emilia is the best swordsman in the land. If you train with her, you will become an equal to any brave knight. Maybe even Sir Lancelot!"

Then Emilia asks, "What about this computer science you spoke of. What kind of science is that? Is it a form of alchemy?" I reply that a computer is a ciphering machine that can be used for many purposes. One can use it make complicated mathematical calculations. It can be used to instantly communicate with others even if they're on the other side of the world. One can also share information with others using a computer. In my job, I program the computer to create imaginary worlds where anything is possible. The characters and worlds they live in are not real, but many ordinary humans still enjoy escaping into those worlds as a diversion from everyday life."

Emilia replies, "So, you could create a world like this one on your computer?"

"Yes. But it would not be real. I'm beginning to believe that this world is real. You are real and so is Grimalkin!"

"Robert, I'm glad you feel that way. I'm so happy that we have met today. But it's probably time for you to return to your world now. We will meet again soon and begin your training. Good night, Robert."

The last thing that I remember is looking into Emilia's green eyes. In another moment I'm no longer in the throne room.

The Mansion

I open my eyes and I can see that I'm once again in the master bedroom of my mansion in Mountain View. I climb out of bed and look out the window at the pool area and back yard. What I see is startling. Sitting on a chair under an umbrella by the pool is Emilia dressed in her warrior queen clothing. Sitting in her lap is Grimalkin. She's gently stroking Grimalkin's long black hair and singing to her.

Emilia notices me in the window. She smiles and says, "Hello Robert! We just decided to drop by and visit."

I tell Emilia that I will be down in a minute. I quickly put on a t-shirt and shorts and then run down to the pool. I pull up a chair next to Emilia. Then I ask, "So, what are you really doing here?" Emilia looks at me with her green eyes and replies, "I would like to learn more about you and the world you live in. It's quite different from either Ragnar or Lancelot's world. Grimalkin tells me that great machines are commonplace here."

I reply, "I will be happy to show you both around, but I do have a question first. Emilia, I know that Grimalkin can make herself invisible to humans and animals. Are you also invisible to them?"

Emilia replies, "Of course not! My powers don't include invisibility. But I can transform into a dragon or a few other creatures."

I explain that Emilia's current clothing will attract too much attention. I say, "Walking around with chain mail armor and a long sword will likely attract the police. It's not a good idea unless we're going to a costume party."

"Robert, do you have suitable clothing for me to wear?"

"Let's go upstairs and try on some of my clothes. We're about the same height. I think I have some clothes that may fit you."

So, we go upstairs into the master bedroom. I was thinking that I'd pick out a pair of shorts and a t-shirt for Emilia, then leave the room briefly so she could change into them in private. It turns out that as soon as we're in the room, her warrior clothes vanish off her body. I'm left speechless. Emilia is standing in front of me completely naked. Emilia's body is stunning. I'm just standing there gawking at her.

Emilia breaks the silence and says, “Robert, you are acting as if you have never seen a woman naked before?” I reply, “Oh! Yes! I have seen a few women naked, but not one who looks quite like you!” She smiles and says, “I will take that as a complement! So, what about the clothes?”

I reply, “Oh, yes. The clothes!” I begin rummaging through my dresser and closet. I pull out a pair of shorts and nervously hold them up to Emilia. She keeps smiling at me. I’m sure she’s enjoying my discomfort. I say, “I think this will fit. It has a belt if an adjustment is needed. She quickly pulls on the shorts, tightens the belt, and says, “That fits nicely.”

I still cannot take my eyes off Emilia. She asks, “Is there a shirt that goes with this?” I reply, “Oh yes!” Then I pull out a light blue t-shirt. She puts it on and steps in front of the mirror.

“How do I look?”

“Beautiful!”

“Thank you, Robert!”

All through this, Grimalkin has been sitting on the bed, quietly watching us. She walks up to Emilia and meows. Emilia pats her head and replies, “Thank you for your approval, Grimalkin!”

I then ask, “Are either of you hungry?” Grimalkin replies, “I don’t eat much.” I give Emilia a questioning look. She answers, “Yes Robert, I do require occasional nourishment.”

I usher everyone downstairs to the kitchen. Emilia watches as I break some eggs and pour the yokes into a pan. I put the pan on one of the burners on the electric stove. Emilia asks, “There is no flame? How are you heating the eggs? I don’t see any wood being kindled.” I reply, “This is an electric stove. The stove operates with electricity. I can explain electricity while we’re eating.”

Emilia looks at the various appliances and asks, “Do these all require electricity to operate?” I respond, “Yes.” She says, Robert, your world appears quite magical to me.”

After breakfast, I suggest that we go to Castro Street in downtown Mountain View. I tell Emilia that on this street you will find many restaurants and small stores and markets. There are also apartment and office buildings nearby. She asks what manner of transportation we will be using. I tell her that we will ride there in my SUV. Again, Emilia gives me a questioning look. I respond by explaining that an SUV is a kind of automated vehicle powered by gasoline, electricity, or a combination of both. We don't typically use horses and carriages to get around anymore. Horse riding has become a recreational activity for some people who can afford to board them at a stable. Horses are also raced as a sport.

We enter my Toyota Rav4 SUV. Emilia is looking around nervously from inside the vehicle. She taps her nails on the glass and says, "Excellent quality. No flaws that I can see. You must have excellent glass makers. Did humans create this glass? In the White Castle, our dwarfs make all the glass, weapons, and armor as well. But they cannot match the clarity of this glass. I explain that in my world, glass is made in factories using precision manufacturing processes. Artisans still make glass manually, but It's mostly for display purposes.

I press the start button. The SUV turns on. I put the SUV in drive, and it begins rolling forward. I pull out of the driveway onto the street. We pass numerous cars traveling in the opposite direction. As we move along, I explain that most people in my world get around in cars and SUVs. Others ride bicycles. Emilia finds all of it fascinating. She says, "I like this world that you live in. In many ways, magic has become a reality."

Just then, we pass a homeless man pushing a grocery cart with his belongings in it. He has an unkept and haggard look about him. Emilia comments, "I see that not everything has changed for the better." I reply, "There are many who have been left behind by the progress in technology. Some end up being homeless and living on the streets."

We park my Rav4 in a lot and begin walking towards Castro Street. I'm wearing a backpack with the top opened so that Grimalkin can comfortably sit inside and stick her head out. Of course, no one that we pass can see her due to her invisibility. Even the dogs that people are walking don't sense her presence. After a few minutes, I notice that Grimalkin is fast asleep inside the backpack.

Emilia immediately takes notice of the ethnic mix of people walking on the street. She asks, "Where did all these people come from? I reply, that over the last few hundred years, people came to the United States from all over the world. Emilia asks why they came here? I reply that they came for many reasons.

Some were slaves, brought against their will. Others came to escape oppression in their home countries. Still others came for the economic opportunities presented in this country." This seems to impress Emilia. She says, "I have been to many of the kingdoms of the world. I recognize the same people here. They seem to get along."

We stop in front of a Chinese curio and herb shop. There are numerous statues of dragons on display. A large dragon poster advertising a local festival is hanging in the window. I ask, "Emilia, could any of these be depictions of you?" She nods her head in the affirmative then says," I visited the country that you call China as a dragon. I was sometimes called Azure, but I was also given other names as well. There were many other dragons that I met in China. Some were my friends; a few were not so nice. Back then, there were many dragons flying around in China. The people worshiped us."

A few stores down the street, there is another poster. This one is for the Disney movie, "Mulan." Emilia says, "Long ago when visiting China, I also took female form, one of my names was Mulan. The people considered me a great warrior." At this point, I'm not surprised by what Emilia has said. I reply, "It appears that you are still remembered. There have been books, movies and plays written about a famous female warrior by that name." Emilia has a big smile on her face. She's quite pleased that she has had such a lasting impact on human history. She says, "The humans of China were very fond of me."

We continue to walk down the street towards the Mountain View transit center. The transit center has a platform for trains and light rail. The lights at the train crossing begin flashing and we can hear loud warning sounds. A train barrels into the station and comes to a halt. Passengers get on and off the train. Then the train whistle blows, and the train gets underway towards its next stop. Emilia is very impressed. She says, "Your world appears to be very organized. Even the common people can move about freely. I don't see any sentries checking them before boarding the train."

Moments later, Emilia notices an object flying high up in the sky. Unlike a hawk or eagle, the object has stationary wings. She turns towards me and asks, "Is this yet another of your transportation machines?" I explain that many people prefer to travel long distances in flying machines called airplanes. There are many types of airplanes from small privately owned ones to very large ones that can carry hundreds of people."

A few minutes later, a fighter jet roars through the sky at a very fast speed. It's likely headed to Moffet Field, a nearby military base. Emilia remarks that this airplane is different from the other ones. It has an intimidating look about it.

I explain that some airplanes are used for military purposes. She asks, "Are those your modern-day dragons?" I reply, "Yes, you can say that. Our military planes carry weapons that can unleash great destruction. We also have ground and ocean-based weapons systems that can do the same."

Emilia comments, "I see that your world is both marvelous and dangerous at the same time. It must be terrible when adversaries clash with machines that carry such destructive power." I agree with her. She says, "A dragon may not be very effective fighting one of those military machines." I find Emilia to be a quick study.

For the rest of the afternoon, we visit various points of interest. Emilia is very excited when we visit San Jose Airport. She's amazed at all of the airplanes taking off and landing. I explain that thousands of people that are being transported to destinations around the country and the world every day.

After visiting the airport, I suggest that we go to the beach. Emilia and Grimalkin both express excitement at getting to see the ocean.

Capitola

We take highway 17 over the Santa Cruz Mountains. The highway winds up over the mountains and emerges in the town of Scotts Valley which is about five miles from the coastal city of Santa Cruz. Santa Cruz is also known by its moniker, Surf City, USA. From Santa Cruz, we drive up the coast a few miles to the picturesque coastal town of Capitola. It's Saturday, so the town is crowded. I park the Rav4 in a remote lot and we begin walking through the town towards the beach. Emilia is excited to see all of the boutique clothing stores. The windows display all sorts of beach clothing for women. She comments on how stylish they are. She also says, "I don't see any clothing for warriors or weapons in these stores. This must be a peaceful place."

Emilia also notices all of the families walking along the street towards the beach. She says, "This place appears to be attractive for human families." Then she asks, "What are those flat objects that many of the children are carrying?" I reply, "Those are boogie boards. The kids and some adults use them to ride ocean waves." A young couple walk past carrying long surfboards." Emilia asks, "Are those adult boogie boards?" I reply, "Those are called surfboards. One can catch a wave and stand up on the surfboard. The wave pushes the surfboard while the rider gets a fun ride. When we reach the main beach, there is an area where you will see many people riding the waves on boogie boards and surfboards."

We reach the esplanade, or walkway, that runs along the beach. We can see hundreds of people relaxing on beach under umbrellas and canopies. Surfboards, boogie boards and beach towels are scattered everywhere. Some groups of people have tables spread out under tents. The tables are covered with food and drinks. Everyone appears to be having a good time.

Emilia says, "It appears that in the human world, leisure is an important pastime. These people are all here to enjoy the warm weather and the ocean." I reply, "Most people work very hard at their jobs during the work week. When the weekend comes, they're ready for some fun. The beach is a popular place to visit."

We reach a jetty protruding out into the bay. On the left side of the jetty, the waves are perfect for riding waves. Emilia watches as the surfers' paddle and catch waves. She says, “That looks like a lot of fun. I would like to try it! Can we acquire a surfboard? Can you teach me how to surf?”

I tell Emilia that I will buy her and myself swimsuits at one of the stores. Then we will rent surfboards at the kiosk located on the beach. Grimalkin has since woken up and taken a peek at the beach activity. She asks, “Do cats surf here too?” I tell her that if she wants, she can ride on the front of my surfboard. I ask her to maintain her invisibility. I don’t want to attract too much attention. Cats on surfboards are a rare sight.

We go into one of the beachwear shops and pick out some swimsuits. Emilia begins to take off her clothes in the middle of the store. I stop her before she gets too far along. I explain that she needs to change in one of the changing rooms. I point to where they’re located. Emilia enters the changing room. I stand guard at the door. I realize that it will take a bit of time to get Emilia acclimated to societal attitudes about nudity in public. I’m also thinking that next time we should visit a nude beach!

Soon we’re both dressed in new swimsuits. I must say that Emilia looks spectacular in her bikini thong swimsuit! I go to the cashier to pay for the suits and a couple of towels. Emilia says, "Robert, I can pay for the clothing." She pulls out a bag and shows it too me. The bag is full of pure silver and gold coins. I respond, "Emilia, in our modern world, gold and silver carry great value. Many people use them for investment purposes. However, we don't use them for daily commerce. We use a currency that we call dollars. In fact, most of our dollars are not physical things. Emilia responds, "Don't tell me. Do keep track of your dollars on your computers?" I respond, "Correct. And we use plastic cards with numbers on them to do the transaction. The credit cards are linked electronically to our bank accounts. Don't worry, I have plenty of dollars in my account." She replies, "Then what good are silver and gold if you cannot buy things with them?" I reply, "If you want to change some of your silver and gold into dollars, we can go to a coin shop. They specialize in buying gold and silver coins and exchanging them for dollars based on the type of coin, its weight, and the current market conditions. We can do that later on. Right now, let's go to the beach and have some fun!"

Our next stop is at a surfboard kiosk located on the walkway next to the beach. It's also in front of the bathrooms and public changing areas. Emilia immediately begins attracting attention. Especially from the male surfers. As I said earlier, Emilia looks spectacular in her bathing suit.

I select an eight-foot-long beginners board for Emilia and a seven-foot board for myself. I happen to be an intermediate level surfer and have taken newbies surfing before. So, I know how to get them started. We put our surfboards down on the sand. I give Emilia a quick lesson on paddling up to a wave and standing up on the board. Emilia thanks me but says, "I figured it out by watching the surfers. It looks pretty easy. Let's go catch some waves!"

I have learned to never doubt what Emilia tells me. So, we enter the water, lie down on our boards, and paddle out to a wave. Grimalkin is sitting on the front end of my surfboard. A moment later a wave approaches. Emilia positions her board perfectly, begins paddling and is quickly up on her board, riding the wave. She begins laughing and says, "This is really fun!" I catch a wave too. Soon we're paddling back out to catch the next wave.

Emilia notices some surfers on shorter boards doing tricks. She asks, "Can I get one of those boards? I want to try the tricks." Once again, I don't question Emilia. So, we paddle back to the beach. At the Kiosk we exchange her eight-foot beginners board for a shorter six-and-a-half-foot epoxy board. We paddle back out again. It takes three wipeouts before Emilia is able to stand up on the shorter board, but when she does, she begins to imitate the tricks being done by other more advanced surfers. Soon she's carving on the front of waves. The other surfers are noticing her. They're clapping and whistling.

All this while, Grimalkin has been sitting on the front of my board. She's maintaining her invisibility. She has been quiet up until now, but then she spots something moving through the water nearby. I turn to see what she's looking at. It's a pod of a dozen or so dolphins swimming about fifty feet away from us. They're propelling themselves through the water, occasionally leaping out and then back into the water. Grimalkin says, "Robert, I'm going to make some friends. Don't worry about me. I will return soon." Having said that, she leaps into the water in the direction of the dolphins. I'm immediately concerned because I cannot see her anywhere in the water. I know that she's a good swimmer, but this is the ocean, not a backyard pool.

Then I notice a solitary black colored dolphin swimming towards the pod. Emilia is sitting on her surfboard next to me. She says, "Robert, don't worry about Grimalkin. She can change form into several different creatures. Dolphins are one of her favorites!" I'm watching Grimalkin join the pod. Immediately she's leaping into air and swimming with them. Emilia says, "She'll swim with them for a while and then come back." Once again, I'm amazed by the abilities of my magical companions. They never cease to amaze me!

Emilia and I continue to surf for the next hour. It's getting a bit late and time to paddle back in and return the surfboards to the kiosk before it closes. I'm looking around for Grimalkin. Then I see the black dolphin swimming up to my board. An instant later it leaps out of the water. Grimalkin materializes on my surfboard. She says, "That was a fun pod of dolphins. They had all sorts of stories to tell me about swimming in this bay. They invited me to join them anytime I'm at the beach!" I look at Emilia and tell her that it's time to paddle back in. After returning the surfboards at the kiosk, we dry ourselves off and change back into our clothes. I make sure to direct Emilia to the women's changing room. Then we return to the Rav4 and drive back over highway 17 to Mountain View. Emilia tells me that she had a wonderful time. Grimalkin is fast asleep in the back seat.

That evening, Emilia and Grimalkin decide to stay the night at the mansion. I begin preparing the guest bedroom for Emilia. She makes a face at me and says that she was rather hoping to stay in the master bedroom with me. She looks at me with her big green eyes and says, "I hope that's ok with you?" My heart is pounding. I responds, "Sure, that's ok with me." I tell her that I'm going to take a shower before getting in bed. I enter the bathroom, remove my clothes, turn on the water and step inside the shower. A moment later, Emilia slips in besides me. Needless to say, my excitement is quite evident. She says, "Robert, thank you for showing me and Grimalkin around your world today." She brings her lips up to mine and we kiss deeply. This turns out to be the most exciting shower of my life. When we finally emerge from the bathroom, I see that Grimalkin is sleeping on a cushion at the base of the bed. "Emilia says, "Don't mind Grimalkin. She likes to sleep a lot. After all, she's a cat."

At this point, I'm all into this fantasy. I wonder what Grimalkin and Emilia have in store for me next!

Flying

I fall asleep with Emilia lying beside me. I believe that I'm dreaming, but I don't feel or see anything. Or am I inside a cloud? Suddenly, I have the sensation that I'm floating in the deep blue sky. I can see the ground far below me. I should be terrified, but for some reason, I'm not.

Off in the distance I can see an object quickly approaching me. The object has wings. As it approaches, I recognize that it's a dragon. In fact, it's Emilia in her dragon body. The Emilia dragon flies directly underneath me. I hear Emilia's voice saying, "Robert, reach for the spines on my back." So, I reach down and grab one of the spines. "Her head turns around and looks at me. I recognize Emilia's fiery green eyes. She says, "Settle in between two of the spines, wrap your hands and legs around them and hold on tight. We're going for a ride!" I ask, "Emilia, where are we going?" She replies, "For a tour of my world!"

Emilia continues flying in a straight line for now. I can feel her dragon body moving up and down with each flap of her powerful wings. The feeling of flight is quite remarkable. The only problem is that the air is blowing into my eyes and blurring my vision. I suspect that Emilia's dragon eyes must have an adaptation for wind.

Emilia says, "Robert, hold on tightly now! We're going down!" We begin a dive. I can see a lake below us. It's very large and blue in color. I begin to wonder if she intends to dive directly into the lake with me on her back. When Emilia is about twenty feet above the lake, she breaks off the dive and begins skimming along the top of the water. It's absolutely exhilarating and at the same time, terrifying experience. She even drags her feet gently across the top of the water, creating a line that marks our path. Then she suddenly rises up into the air once more. I look below and see that a giant sea serpent has launched itself out of the water in a desperate attempt to capture Emilia in its jaws. It ends up snapping at empty air instead. Emilia is long gone. The serpent crashes back into the water. Emilia says, "The old sea serpent always falls for that trick. I probably should not tease it that way, but its fun to see it try so hard to catch me!" I'm thinking that this fantasy world appears to have its fill of perils.

On the far side of the lake, I can see a heard of large creatures grazing on tall grass. They look a lot like duck billed dinosaurs. I ask. "Emilia, do you have dinosaurs in this world?" She replies, "Oh, yes. We have many of the species that used to live in your world a very long time ago. In your world they perished, but not here." We briefly circle around the dinosaur herd. There must be at least two hundred of them grazing. Smaller dinosaurs are also grazing nearby them.

We continue to fly over lush forests and grassy meadows. The meadows are filled with a variety of creatures grazing on the grass. Some are dinosaurs, others are mammals. It's an idyllic scene. We circle around one large meadow. I can see huge rodent type creatures and a couple of triceratops. The triceratops were my favorite childhood dinosaur. Now I'm getting to see them up close! Emilia senses my interest and continues to circle around the meadow.

A moment later I hear a roar emanating from the forest at the far corner of the meadow. A large creature resembling a tyrannosaurus emerges. The creatures that were grazing in the meadow all turn to see the intruder. In an instant, they take off in a panic. The tyrannosaurus immediately begins perusing them. One large boar falls behind the others. The tyrannosaurus quickly falls upon it. The boar is caught in the huge jaws of the monster. It squeals and kicks its legs in an effort to escape. But It's too late. The monster's powerful jaws tear into the body of the hapless boar. In moments, the boar is stripped of its most fleshy parts and only the skeleton, tendons and inner organs are left. As the tyrannosaurus moves on, a flock of vultures and Pteranodons descend on the remains of the boar. One creature has remained in the meadow, unmoved by the presence of the tyrannosaurus. It's a triceratops. As the tyrannosaurus approaches, the triceratops turns to face it. The tyrannosaurus raises its head, gnashes its teeth and roars loudly. In response, the triceratops swings its formidable horns from side to side and lets out a less formidable whistling sound. Nonetheless, the triceratops has signaled that It's not intimidated by the intruder.

The tyrannosaurus begins a series of false attacks, in an effort to feel out the defenses of the triceratops. The triceratops reacts to each move with a defensive move, always pointing its sharp horns in the direction of the tyrannosaurus. It becomes apparent that this encounter will end in a stalemate. Perhaps the tyrannosaurus, having already consumed a boar, is thinking that it's not worth risking injury should the triceratops manage to gore it with one of its three horns. A few moments later the tyrannosaurus turns and begins to exit the meadow. Just before it reaches the forest it turns around and lets out one last mighty roar. Then it disappears from sight. The triceratops turns back to munching on the grass as though nothing unusual has transpired. Slowly, the other creatures begin returning to the meadow.

I have just witnessed one of the most exciting dinosaur confrontations possible. As a child, I would act out this same confrontation with my toy dinosaurs. But this confrontation appears to be real! Or is it? This could easily have been a part of a video game that I created when I worked at Arbak Gaming.

As we fly over the treetops of the forest, I can see several objects approaching us. As they get closer, it become obvious what they are. I ask Emilia, “More dragons?” Emilia replies, “Did you think that I was the only one?” Soon we’re at the center of a flock of dragons. Most are smaller and less formidable looking that Emilia. I can hear them chatting amongst themselves. They seem to be paying particular attention to what Emilia is saying. I ask Emilia, “Are you, their leader?” She replies, “I’m their queen!”

“So, what are all these dragons doing here?”

"They're guarding the lands around the White Castle. Dragons are the first line of defense. In our world, dragons carry out a function similar to your military airplanes."

"Who are they guarding against."

"The evil ones."

"Who are the evil ones? Where are they?"

"The evil ones have always been with us. They live far to the east in a land of darkness. They covet the White Castle. They want to capture it and control the portals."

"The portals?"

"The White Castle contains numerous portals into your human world. Your bedframe is but one of them."

"Emilia, you mean to tell me that the bed frame that I sleep on at night, is actually a portal connecting this world to the one that I live in?"

"Robert, I think that statement sums it up. You are sleeping on a portal!"

"Wow!"

Emilia decides that we have had enough flying for today, so we head back towards the White Castle. When we arrive at the gate, Emilia transforms back into her human warrior queen body. The gate opens and Grimalkin is there to greet us. She says, "It looks like you kids had some fun flying around today!"

Emilia replies, "I gave Robert the grand tour of the lands surrounding the White Castle. Perhaps its time for you to show Robert some more of the inside of the castle. I also told Robert about the portals."

I add, "I'm very interested in the portals because apparently one of them leads directly to my bedroom! I'm cool with you and Emilia visiting me but being paid a visit by evil ones is a bit scary! What are the evil ones anyway."

Grimalkin says, "There exists an evil sorcerer named Lord Malvus, who presently lives in the east. He wields great power. He also has a host of minions at his command. Those minions are often summoned by Lord Malvus to carry out various nefarious deeds."

"Can Lord Malvus and his minions find their way into my bedroom?"

"Not if we can keep them away from the White Castle. You see, Lord Malvus once had control of the White Castle. He abused the portals by sending his evil minions into your human world. They spread their evil throughout many of the lands in the human world. Emilia and other good dragons were sent to your world to defeat and capture the evil ones and bring them back to our world.

In the human world, the dragons allied themselves with the great sorcerer, Merlin. After many centuries of confrontation, Lord Malvus and his minions were forced back into our world through the portals. In the aftermath of a great battle fought inside the White Castle itself, Lord Malvus and his minions were driven back to the dark, forbidden lands of the east. Lord Malvus settled into the Dark Castle and has been plotting his return ever since. His minions include gargoyles, goblins, ogres, and other evil entities. Lord Malvus often puts a spell on a crow and orders it to fly over the White Castle to spy on us."

Emilia adds, "Lord Malvus has recently been using dark magic that allows a gargoyle to falsely take on the appearance of a small dragon. Several penetrated our defenses but were stopped short of accomplishing their mission to steal portal artifacts from the White Castle. To combat the false dragons, we dragons have developed a verbal code system to positively identify each other."

I comment, "Wow, you guys are practicing security strategies. Be careful though because any security scheme, no matter how clever, can be defeated. Maybe I can help the dragons come up with a more foolproof scheme. After all, I'm a computer programmer with experience in security. To start with, you could change the code every day."

I look at Grimalkin and ask, "What about security inside the White Castle? How would the cats resist if Lord Malvus's minions reach the White Castle?

Grimalkin responds that felines can be ferocious if they choose to be. She says, "Let me demonstrate!" I look at her small cat body with skepticism. Then a remarkable transformation occurs. Grimalkin's cat body begins to blur and undulate. A larger body quickly takes form. When the transformation is complete, I'm staring at a large ferocious black panther. Grimalkin lets out a terrifying shrill cry. I respond by saying, “Oh! I guess that answers my question!”

Grimalkin reverts back to her cat form. Then she says, “We cats transform into panthers and other predatory felines should the need arise to defend the White Castle. We also have other magical tricks we can unleash upon an intruder. That’s how we and the dragons chased Lord Malvus and his minions from the White Castle long ago. We also enlisted the help of Merlin. Merlin is the most powerful sorcerer of all. If necessary, we will do it once more. But to be sure, Lord Malvus is clever and resourceful. No doubt he has been at work preparing a surprise for us.”

I ask, “So were do I fit in all of this?” Emilia responds. “We will find out soon enough!”

The White Castle Tour

Grimalkin leads Emilia and I through the White Castle. The stalls that were empty in a previous dream, are now filled with dwarfs and elves. They're busily going about the business of commerce. This looks like a village marketplace scene from Lord of The Rings! It appears that the dwarfs specialize in smithing. Their shops display an array of swords, axes, shields and even armor. One stall has a display of jewelry. Many elves can be seen looking at their wares.

The elves appear to be working in the shops where fine clothing, carpets and other products made of textiles are on display. The dwarfs and elves seem to be getting along with each other. I was hoping to see a hobbit or two, but I guess they only exists in the imagination!

Next, we visit a series of chambers on the main floor of the castle. Here we find rooms full of cats milling about. Grimalkin says that the cats tend to roam throughout the castle and take naps whenever and wherever they please.

Soon we enter a courtyard. Here I see that the cats have transformed into leopards, panthers, and tigers. They're practicing their fighting skills. In one area, the big felines pounce upon each other and wrestle around. This appears to be hand to hand combat training, feline style.

A kind of obstacle course is set up where the felines climb structures, leap across gaps and race around obstacles. Grimalkin comments that all felines in the White Castle must undergo transformation and fitness training on a regular basis. "We're required to be prepared to fight if called upon to do so." To my eye, this looks like a military boot camp.

We go back inside the castle and enter a large, cavernous room. Here another form of training is occurring.

A large gray-haired cat is standing in the middle of the room meowing at a group of cats. The cats are taking turns raising their right front paws and firing off bolts of energy at stone targets positioned along the walls of the cavern. The energy blasts remind me of magic wand battle scenes from the Harry Potter movies.

Grimalkin says, “The large gray cat is Master Merval. Merval is Merlin’s favorite feline. Merlin passed much of his knowledge to Merval. Merval presently serves as the master trainer for the magic arts. The felines in this room are advanced in their magical skills. They have learned how to channel their psychic energy into a physical manifestation. In this case it has taken the form of a bolt of energy that’s aimed at a spot on the stone targets.” I can see by the burn marks on the targets that this can be a formidable weapon if used against an adversary. I watch carefully as each cat focuses on a spot on the target and then delivers a bolt of energy from their extended paw. I guess they don’t require a magic wand to channel the energy! A furry paw seems to do the trick!

Grimalkin lets out a short meow. This catches Merval’s attention. Merval walks over to us. I can feel Merval’s thoughts enter into my mind. He too is telepathic!

Merval says, “Robert, I’m very happy to meet you. Grimalkin has told me about you. She says that you have much promise for a human. We shall see about that. If you are agreeable, I will serve as your magic arts instructor. I can teach you the art of channeling your psychic energy to manipulate the physical environment around you. My master, Merlin, taught me how to do this. I can teach you."

I find myself almost speechless. I'm to be trained on how to do real magic! Once more, fantasy is becoming reality. I respond, "Master Merval, I would be honored to have you as my teacher."

There, I have done it! I'm fully committed to becoming part of this fantasy world. If I have gone crazy, then so be it. I'm living every imaginative child's dream. This is better that virtual reality! It's one hundred percent real! Or is it?

Grimalkin says, "Let's continue the tour." We exit the cavern and climb up a winding stairway to the floor above. After walking down, a narrow hallway, we enter a room. In the center is a bedframe not unlike my own. There is no mattress. Its simply a headboard and a footboard connected by two rails. Both the headboard and a footboard have a red gemstone embedded in them.

Grimalkin comments, "Robert, this bed frame is a portal that connects directly to the bed fame in your bedroom. Both Emilia and I have used it to move back and forth between our world and yours. This is but one portal of many in the White Castle. In each room along this corridor there is yet another portal. Some are inoperative because the other end of the portal has been lost or destroyed. Yours became active when you reconstructed the bedframe and began sleeping in the bed."

As we enter each room, I see a variety of objects that are portals. Three of them are mirrors. I recall fables about magical mirrors. I guess this must be the basis for those mirror fables.

Other portals include a walk-in dresser, a bathtub, a window frame, a door and several ancient looking chairs and couches. Grimalkin did not say where each portal leads to. She does say that there is one special portal that can project someone to anywhere inside this world. That said, It's a one-way portal. Once you pass through it, you must find your way back. She says, "It's to be used wisely, or not at all. This portal requires a special incantation to be activated using a crystal ball. Only Merlin knows the words of the incantation. He has not yet decided to pass this incantation on to anyone else, not even Merval. Merlin is so stubborn! He keeps saying, "When the time comes, I will pass the last of my knowledge on."

I ask, so where is Merlin now? I heard that he lives in a tower. There are many towers in the White Castle. Which one does he live in?"

Grimalkin replies, "Merlin lives in the central tower. He keeps his crystal ball in his quarters. The tower is located in the center of the White Castle. Merlin mostly keeps to himself, but sometimes descends to the throne room at night. Merval is the only cat that he allows inside his quarters. That's how he finds out what is happening in the outside world. Merlin is a most eccentric sorcerer."

I reply, "I would like to meet him sometime. He was one of my favorite characters when I was growing up. I would like to hear about his times in King Arthur's Court."

Grimalkin says, "You will get your chance when he feels fit to meet you. In the meantime, we must return to the training room. Merval will be conducting your first magic arts lesson."

Emilia then says, "After that, I will be teaching you the art of sword fighting! And maybe archery too."

Training

Grimalkin and I re-enter the training room. Master Merval is curled up on a cushion on the floor. The other felines have left. Merval rises up, stretches, and lets out a meow. He walks over to us and telepathically greets me, “Welcome Robert. This will be your first day of practice. We will begin by doing a relaxation exercise. Please take a sitting position on the cushion. Close your eyes and relax. Begin to notice your breathing.”

I reply, “This is similar to the meditation that I do each morning.” Merval replies, “Very good.” After a while, I begin to feel my mind drift. Merval places some thoughts in my mind. He tells me to imagine an object, a small ball, floating in space. He instructs me to focus my mind on the ball then begin to move it around. Merval the says, “Open your eyes Robert, but remain seated and relaxed. Notice the ball in the far corner of the room. Whisper this incantation and focus your mental energy on the ball. Try and move it.”

Merval then tells me the incantation. I repeat it softly in my mind. I’m completely focused on the ball. Suddenly it begins to move slightly. I’m actually moving the ball! Merval tells me to not break my concentration. The ball begins moving some more.

Merval says, "Robert, that was very good. Grimalkin was correct to bring you here to the White Castle. You have the gift. We will continue your training tomorrow. I believe that Emilia is waiting in the training yard to begin your physical training.

Having said that, Merval walks over to the cushion, lies down and is soon fast asleep. I have to remind myself that Merval may be a great wizard, but he's still a cat. Cats sleep twelve to sixteen hours a day. All through the castle, I see cats napping in just about any place they find space to lie down. I have to watch my step and not trip over one of them.

When I reach the training yard, Emilia is waiting for me. She greets me with a wide smile. Emilia is wearing her warrior chain mail with the dragon image emblazoned on the front. She says, "Hello Robert. Are you ready to begin your sword fight training? You know that It's an important skill that must be mastered before becoming a knight." I nod my head then ask, "Will I receive cool chain mail armor like yours? Emilia says, "If you master the techniques, yes." Then she hands me a blunted long sword. It's not unlike the swords that we used at the medieval club I joined in college. She says, "For now you can put that aside. We will not be using the sword today. Instead, we will begin with some basic footwork. Footwork is critical to sword fighting." Emilia begins demonstrating some foot movements.

I try my best to do the drills that Emilia is teaching me. It's hard to keep pace with her because she's so quick and effortless in her movements. After about thirty minutes I'm beginning to tire. Emilia notices this and says, "Lets move on to something else." She says that It's time to measure my arm strength. She tells me to hold my arms out in front of my body and resist the downward pressure she exerts on them. Emilia is easily able to push my arms down despite my resistance. She's much stronger than I originally thought.

She says, "I think that we need to work on your arm and core strength." So, Emilia begins putting me through a series of strength drills. Soon, I'm doing pushups and knee bends holding a heavy rock in my arms. I must admit that Emili is a pretty tough trainer.

After another hour she says, "That's enough for the physical training for today. I'm going to demonstrate a number of sword fighting drills for you before we call it quits. I sit attentively and watch as Emilia executes each movement with grace and skill. She explains the purpose of each drill. Emilia is amazing. Back home, she would be considered a super athlete. Emilia says, “We will try some of these moves tomorrow. Why don’t we relax a bit.” She gives me a sly smile. She takes my hand and leads me out of the courtyard. Soon we’re in the main courtyard of the White Castle. Emilia steps back a few feet and transforms into her dragon body. Soon, this gigantic fire breathing dragon is standing where Emilia once stood. She lays one of her wings down on the ground and says, “Climb aboard Robert!” I begin climbing up her wing and onto her back. I ask, “Where are we going?” Emilia responds, “Somewhere special. It’s a surprise!”

In a moment, we’re airborne. Emilia begins flying south over the forest towards the nearby foothills. After flying over the first set of hills, she dives downward into a valley. I can see the lush landscape below us. A beautiful small lake appears. She sets down at a clearing on the shore of the lake. Emilia transforms back into her human form. She takes my hand, and we begin walking along the shoreline of the lake. Soon we approach a sheer rock face. I can see a waterfall running down the rocks and emptying into the lake. There is a cavern partially hidden behind the waterfall. The scenery is absolutely breathtaking. It reminds me a bit of some of the waterfalls on the island of Maui.

Emilia turns to me and says, “This is one of my favorite places.” She gives me a kiss. Then she removes her clothing and dives into the water. She surfaces and waves to me. “Come on in. The water is great!” I ask, “Is there anything swimming around in the water that I should know about?” She laughs and says, “Just me and a few fish! They may nibble at you a bit!”

So, I remove my clothes and dive in after her. Soon we’re splashing and swimming after each other in the cool water. Yes, it’s a bit cold, but I don’t care because I’m with Emilia. If I get hypothermia, she’ll save me.

We swim over to the waterfall. There is a large flat rock underneath it, so we stand there enjoying the water pounding in our bodies. Emilia then takes my hand, and we walk through the waterfall and into the cavern behind it.

We’re inside the cavern now. It’s fantastic! I see stalactites hanging from the roof of the cavern and stalagmites protruding upwards. There is also an eerie luminescence emanating from the interior of the cavern. I look at Emilia. Our eyes lock. Once again, I'm lost inside of her bright green eyes. She leads me out of the water to a flat rock shelf. We lie down together, and our lips meet. Soon we're intertwined in a passionate embrace.

I lose track of how long we have been there. We're lying side by side staring up at the ceiling of the cavern. The last thing that I recall is Emilia whispering in my ear, "Good night my brave magical knight."

The next thing I remember is waking up in my bed in the mansion. I can recall everything that happened. It was totally real! My muscles also are aching. This feeling is not unlike when I have done a hard workout at a gym. My hand feels something next to me in the bed. I pick it up and look at it. It's a piece of stalagmite. I must have had it in my hand when I fell asleep. Or maybe Emilia put it in my hand to reassure me that what I experienced was real!

I get up and go about my usual morning routine. There is still a lot of work to do around the house. The day turns out to be relatively uneventful. No visitation from Grimalkin or Emilia. I finish painting the bedrooms and begin painting the hallway.

For the next few weeks, I return to the White Castle every evening. Emilia and Merval continue my training. Somehow, I'm learning very quickly. Merval teaches me how to focus my mental energy so intensely that I'm now able to create small energy blasts on the targets in the training room. This is facilitated by my holding a stick in my hand. The stick is the medium through which I can project the energy blast. You guessed it! The stick is my magic wand. Merval explains that the stick is simply a prop used in the early stages of training. Once I become proficient at projecting my mental energy, I will no longer require the stick. He says that the cats are all proficient at projecting energy blasts simply by directing their paw at the target. The energy blast is not actually released by the paw. The paw, or a stick is merely an aiming device. The most proficient, don't require using their paw at all. They just apply psychic energy. Merval and Grimalkin are able to do this. Merlin can also accurately project energy blast without a wand or hand pointed at the target. But Merlin does possess mediums that can amplify his psychic energy. These are real magic wands and staffs.

My training with Emilia has also progressed. I'm able to swordfight far more effectively than when

I was in college. She invites several of the dragons to take human form and mock fight with me. This gives me the opportunity to learn to fight opponents of various sizes and skill levels. I even defeat one of the dragons, in human form, in a mock swordfight. Or maybe she was being nice to me!

The Dark Castle

Lord Malvus is staring into his crystal ball. He turns to his gargoyle assistant, Lakees. He says, "Lakees, I can see the White Castle very clearly. My power over the crystal ball has been growing. So has my ability to enter the mind of creatures like the crows. Through their eyes, I'm able to survey the White Castle from the sky.

Lakees replies, "Master, what are you seeing now? Malvus replies, "I can see three dragons flying towards the castle. They're descending down into the center of the White Castle grounds. Oh, I can see more now. They're transforming into their human form. Now there are five human forms in the courtyard. I recognize all but one of the life forms. The dragons all have an aura about them. This fifth one has no aura. It appears to be a human!"

Lakees says, "Master, what is a human doing in the White Castle?"

Lord Malvus replies, "Lakees, until now only felines, dragons, elves, dwarfs, and Merlin have been frequenting the White Castle. This is a new development. I must find out why a human is present in the White Castle! Go now and leave me to ponder this situation!"

Lakees departs. Lord Malvus walks over to the window of his chamber. The chamber is located at the top of the highest tower overlooking his Dark Castle. He looks out over his realm. In the sky, there are hundreds of gargoyles flying about. Below, he can see the army of goblins congregated in encampments both inside and surrounding the outer wall of the castle. Inside the castle grounds, his elite goblin guard are manning their stations. He reflects on the preparations he has been making to retake the White Castle and the precious portals that were stolen from him by the felines, dragons, and Merlin. The dragons and felines are a formidable adversary. That's why he has been building up his armies with more gargoyles and goblins. As for Merlin, he'll deal with him personally!

Lord Malvus's spies, the crows, have been reporting to him regarding the strength of his adversaries. Lord Malvus has been preparing his invasion of the White Castle based solely on the numbers of defending felines and dragons. It's a grim calculation knowing that much of his goblins and gargoyles will be incinerated by dragons and torn apart by the felines. But the numbers are in his favor. He'll win the war of attrition.

The inclusion of humans in the equation is an entirely different question. If human warriors and knights join the side of his enemies, the equation could be tilted against him. There is also the question of Merlin. He has not been seen for months. Was Merlin even alive? Or has he finally succumbed to old age. If alive, does Merlin still possess the powers that he once had?

The risks are great; however, Lord Malvus yearns to recapture the power he once had over this world and the world of humans. He once reigned supreme over both.

It was a time where he could dispatch his minions through portals into the world of the humans. They would corrupt the humans in power and conquer his adversaries in the human world. Kings under his control would dispatch dark knights to slay dragons.

Through trickery, his minions would also set the kingdoms of humans against each other. The hate produced by these rivalries only increased his power over the humans. Soon came waves of disease and pestilence spread by his minions. Malvus's power continued to grow with the chaos his minions created. Lord Malvus thrives on war, disease, and death.

But then Merlin, Emilia, Grimalkin, and the dragons emerged to counter Malvus's forces. They drove most of Lord Malvus's minions out of the human world, through the portals and back into the White Castle. Next, they drove Lord Malvus and his minions out of the White Castle. Malvus was forced to retreat to the Dark Castle. He has been there ever since. With most of his army of gargoyles and goblins destroyed or in disarray, he was forced to retrench and rebuild. It has taken two hundred years, but Lord Malvus has been patient. It has taken a lot of time for his forces to reach their current strength.

Lord Malvus has been sending out raiding parties to test the dragons guarding the area lands surrounding the White Castle. The time is close when Lord Malvus will attack the White Castle and once again control the portals to the human world.

Robert

It's been a long day of digging up the garden and putting down new soil and fertilizer for the spring crop. Now that I have some land of my own, I plan to have a vegetable garden. I have been growing my seedlings in a small greenhouse that's next to the main house. I have planted an assortment of vegetables including beans, Colliflower, Broccoli, Zucchini, Carrots, beets, and cucumbers. I will let the small plants grow for four weeks before transferring them into the soil of the garden. This the first garden that I have planted since childhood back in New York. I'm really excited to see how it turns out!

It's getting late and I'm tired, so I wash up and get into bed. Before I doze off, I wonder what Emilia and Grimalkin have planned for me when I wake up in the White Castle. I soon fall asleep.

Grimalkin

Grimalkin is standing next to the bedframe portal in the White Castle. She utters a series of meows. The red gemstones begin to glow. This commences the portal transfer process. The bedframe in Robert's master bedroom in his mansion will also begin glowing. Robert's sleeping body will begin to fade away. In moments, his body will materialize in the training yard where Emilia and Merval are waiting for him. But something is wrong. The gemstones on the headboard and baseboard begin flickering and seconds later are no longer glowing.

Sensing something unexpected has happened, Grimalkin runs to the training yard to see if Robert has materialized there. When she reaches the yard, she sees Emilia and Merval standing there, but no sign of Robert. She tells them of her concerns. Merval decides to have several of the felines search the castle for Robert. Emilia changes into her dragon form and begins flying around the fields and meadows outside of the castle walls. She cannot find a trace of Robert. Grimalkin decides to travel to Robert's mansion to see if perhaps he's still sleeping in his bed.

Grimalkin returns to the White Castle. All three report that they have not found a trace of Robert anywhere. Grimalkin says, something or someone has manipulated the portal. Merval says, "There can only be one explanation. This is Lord Malvus's doing. Somehow, he has manipulated the portal and diverted Robert away from it's intended destination. Emilia is alarmed at this prospect. She says, "I will alert the dragons to begin searching the fields and forests leading to the Dark Castle. Maybe Robert has materialized in a location within the range of the portal, but still close enough to the Dark Castle that Malvus's minions can capture him. We must depart at once to begin the search!"

The Field

When I wake up, I find myself in a large field. I cannot see the White Castle. Nor do I see Emilia, Grimalkin or any of the felines and dragons. I soon realize that I'm alone. The only sound that I hear is the rustling of tall grass in response to a light breeze. It's a bit unnerving to say the least.

So, I try and take a guess at which direction I should be walking in order to find the White Castle. Besides, sooner or later, one of the dragons will likely spot me when Emilia and Grimalkin realize that I have not shown up at the White Castle.

I continue to walk through the field. I look up at the sky hoping to spot one of the dragons. That's when I notice a group of flying objects headed in my direction. At first, I think that it's the dragons, but there are too many of them. Dragons also tend to space themselves apart. These objects appear more like a flock of geese flying in formation. But I don't hear them making honking sounds as geese usually do.

As the flying objects get closer, I note that they're too large to be birds. In fact, they almost look like humans with wings. I'm beginning to get an uneasy feeling. Finally, the objects are close enough to get a good look at them.

It strikes me that I have seen these flying creatures before. Their statues adorn many medieval buildings. The creatures are gargoyles! They're grotesque, fearsome looking creatures. The first of the gargoyles are close now. I look around for a place where I can hide from them, but there is nothing. I'm trapped in the open. There is no place to run. I resolve that I must stand and face these flying monsters.

In moments, I'm surrounded by dozens of gargoyles. More are arriving every minute. They begin to close in on me. Each one is about three quarters my size, but there are so many of them. I realize that I cannot fight them all off.

One of the larger gargoyles, steps forward. He begins speaking in a hissing, sinister voice reminiscent of Gollum from Lord of The Rings. He says, "Sssss, human, come with us peacefully and we will not harm you. Sssss."

I respond, "Who are you? Where are you going to take me?"

"Sssss, I'm Lakees! We will take you to the Dark Castle to meet our master, Lord Malvus! He has much to discuss with you! Sssss."

"I think not!"

"Sssss, it's your choice human! Peacefully, or by force! Sssss."

I take up a fighting stance to show my defiance. Truthfully, I'm scared to death, but I cannot show it to these winged monsters. My best hope is to keep them busy and hope that Emilia and the dragons spot me.

Lakees says, "Sssss, have it your way human! Sssss!"

The gargoyles begin charging at me. I commence spinning around and throwing kicks at them as they approach me. Several of the gargoyles are struck by my feet and fists. They go flying backwards into their fellow gargoyles. I have the initial upper hand, but then they overcome me by sheer numbers. Despite their sharp looking teeth, they don't bite me. It's obvious that their goal is capture and not injury. Soon, I'm being held firmly by a half dozen or so of the gargoyles. I can feel their claw hands tightening around my arms and legs. I cannot break their grip on me. Lakees says, "Sssss, to the Dark Castle! Sssss.

I'm airborne now. I can feel the gargoyles that are holding me flap their wings. My weight is keeping them from attaining much altitude. We're flying about ten or fifteen feet above the ground. I continue to struggle as long as I'm this far off the ground. A fall from here onto the tall grass is survivable. Surrounding us in flight are Lakees and about one hundred gargoyles.

I can see the Dark Castle off in the distance. It has a menacing look about it. I have the feeling that I really don't want to be there, so I increase my resistance.

Suddenly I hear a loud roar from above me. It's Lola, one of the smaller dragons. She must have spotted the ruckus and decided to intervene. The gargoyles take note and half of them break off to engage Lola in an arial battle. The ones holding me continue on in the direction of the castle.

Lola swoops down at the gargoyles. She lets out a burst of fire from her mouth. This incinerates three of the gargoyles closest to her. This does not deter the others. They keep on coming at her. It's clear that they're buying time for the others to take me to the Dark Castle.

A fierce battle ensues between Lola and the gargoyles. I can see her breathing fire on them and also fighting them off with her tail and powerful wings. Several of the gargoyles are struck and fall to the ground. I can also see two more dragons off in the distance approaching as quickly as they can. But they're very far away.

Lola's effort to fight through the gargoyles is proving fruitless. She's soon out of fire and must rely entirely on her body to fight off the gargoyles. Despite losing half of their numbers, the gargoyles are relentless in attacking her.

The distance between myself and the Dark Castle is closing now. Lakees orders more gargoyles to defend the air space between us and Lola. In moments, the gargoyles have whisked me over the walls and into the courtyard of the castle. While passing over the walls of the Dark Castle, I can see that It's well defended. Large goblins are manning the walls. In addition, there are numerous giant crossbows and catapults mounted on the walls.

These are obviously defenses to be used against an attack on the castle. The crossbows in particular look like a defense against dragons. I sense that I'm in for a rough time. *Can I wake up from this nightmare now?*

Emilia

Lola has succeeded in fighting off the gargoyles that attacked her. She sees me being whisked over the wall of the Dark Castle. When she approaches the Dark Castle, she's greeted by a large arrow shot from one of the giant, wall mounted crossbows. Lola dodges the arrow just in time. It misses her body by less than a foot. She's forced to retreat until the other approaching dragons meet up with her.

Soon there are three dragons gathered a safe distance from the Dark Castle. Dragon's Maisie and Sophie have joined Lola. Lola says, "The gargoyles have Robert!" Sophie asks, "What should we do next?" Lola replies, "We're too few now to attack the Dark Castle. They have giant crossbow weapons that can shoot us out of the sky if we get too close." Maisie responds, "We must go back to the White Castle and let Emilia, Merval and Grimalkin know what has happened. They will have the best idea as to what actions we should take next." The three dragons turn around and fly in direction of the White Castle.

Grimalkin has gathered Emilia, Merval and many of the felines to the throne room. She recounts that Robert was late in arriving at the castle. She sensed that something has gone wrong, “He usually turns up at the castle by now. She describes how she used the portal to visit Robert’s mansion in Mountain View. She searched his entire property, but he was nowhere to be seen. She also observed that his automobile and bicycle were still on the property. This is unusual. Robert is rather disciplined with his daily schedule. You can count on him going to bed on schedule and then showing up here after he passes through the portal.

Lola, Maisie, and Sophie burst into the throne room. Lola says, “I was flying over a field not far from the Dark Castle when I saw a large number of gargoyles congregated in a section of the field. It appeared that there was a struggle of some sort occurring there. Fearing that the gargoyles were up to no good, I flew in to investigate. I could see Robert surrounded by gargoyles. He was attempting to fight them off. Then I saw them overpower Robert and carry him towards the Dark Castle. I attempted to intervene and free Robert but was attacked by a large number of the gargoyles. By the time that I subdued them, Robert was already taken over the castle wall. Maisie and Sophie arrived to help me, but it was too late. Robert was already captured and out of sight.”

Emilia says, “How’s this possible? I thought that the portal only worked between the area immediately surrounding the castle and Robert’s bedroom.”

Merval replies, “I sense Lord Malvus’s hand in this. Malvus has great powers that he can project through his crystal ball. He also has spies flying about the White Castle. Malvus likely became aware of Robert’s presence here and used his crystal ball to alter the portal somehow. This is a grave development indeed.”

Emilia says, “We must free Robert before he comes to harm at the hand of Lord Malvus!” I will fly to the Dark Castle immediately to free him!”

Lola urges caution. She tells the others about the giant wall mounted crossbows and how an arrow from one of them almost struck her.

Grimalkin says, “A full frontal assault will likely result in a great number of casualties. We need to be clever about how we approach this problem. Lord Malvus used sorcery to abduct Robert. Perhaps we should do the same!” Grimalkin looks directly at Merval while she’s saying this.

Merval senses what Grimalkin is asking. He says, "Merlin is indeed the greatest sorcerer of them all. But he's difficult to deal with. Merlin hides in the main tower with his crystal ball. On a few rare occasions he allows me to briefly enter his chamber and speak with him. Most of the time he simply wants to reminisce about the old times in King Arthur's court." Merval looks around at the pleading eyes of Grimalkin and the dragons. Then he says, "All right! I'll do it! I will approach Merlin and ask him to assist us in freeing Robert from the Dark Castle!"

Robert

I have been flown over the wall of the Dark Castle by the gargoyles. The gargoyles drop me on the ground in the middle of castle courtyard. My arms and legs are sore from the pressure exerted on them by the gargoyles. I'm thoroughly exhausted!

Two large, nasty looking goblins grab ahold of each of my arms. Despite my resistance, they drag me along the ground and through a door at the base of a large structure in the center of the Dark Castle.

The goblins continue to drag me down a long corridor. We enter a large room. I can see a tall dark hooded figure standing at the center of the room. There are a dozen well-armed goblins standing nearby. These appear to be guards.

I'm thrown down at the feet of the tall figure. The figure pulls back his hood to reveal a gaunt drawn face with glowing red eyes. The figure begins to speak. It says, "I'm Lord Malvus. This is my Dark Castle. You are my guest!"

I look up at Lord Malvus and ask, "Why have you abducted me? I'm a common human who lacks any special powers. What value could I be to you?"

"Oh, you are of great value to me, Robert! More than you can imagine!"

"How do you know my name?"

"I know a lot of things about you. After all, I'm a sorcerer. I have been tracking your movement between the human world and this one. It was a simple matter to divert your most recent portal transference away from the White Castle and beyond the protection of the dragons. My gargoyles, led by Lakees, did the rest of the work. Now we have you."

"You still have not told me why you want me!"

"Robert, you have powerful friends. And I don't believe that you have been brought to our world for no reason at all. There is more to you than you are leading on to."

Lord Malvus locks his eyes onto mine. I find that I cannot look away from him. His red eyes begin to grow in size. Soon all I can see is his eyes looking into my soul. I try and resist their power. I hear a voice inside my head demanding, "What are you doing here? Tell me!" I continue to resist. My head is spinning. Once again, the questions come, "Why were you brought to the White castle? Did Merlin summon you?" Again, I resist. The pain in my head is growing. I feel that I'm losing control. I say to myself, "Hang on!"

Suddenly Lord Malvus releases me from his spell. He says, "I can see that you will be a difficult one. But I will discover your secret soon enough. We will talk again soon. I have ways to get the information that I require. Even from a difficult one like you. But for the moment, I have more pressing matters to attend to." Lord Malvus looks towards one of the goblins and says, "Take him to the dungeon! Show him some of our hospitality, but don't kill him. I want to continue the interrogation later." Then he abruptly turns around and exits the room.

Once again, I'm dragged out of the room by two goblins. They take me down a spiral staircase into a dank, foul smelling underground cavern. A goblin with a key in his hand greets us. I can see that the cavern is ringed by cells with closely spaced metal rods for walls. There are a strange looking assortment of beings housed in several of the cells. Most are sleeping, or maybe dead. This reminds me of a jail cell block from an old western movie.

The goblins throw me down onto the floor of an empty cell. Then they proceed to kick me in the sides several times. When they're done, they slam the door shut and lock it. The goblins stare in at me and laugh. One of the goblins says, "There won't be much left of this one after Lord Malvus is done with him!" Then he and the other goblin turn and leave. The jailer goblin with the key walks over to a table and sits down.

I'm in pain, but still manage to regain my feet. I realize that the beating could have been worse had Lord Malvus not told them that he wanted me alive.

I look around the cell to see if there is any easy way to get out of it. Three walls are made of stone all the way up to the ceiling. The front is made of closely spaced metal bars. They're spaced too closely for me to slip through them. The goblin jailkeeper is watching me. He says, "No one escapes from the dungeon of the Dark Castle!" He picks up a metal rod and bangs it against the cage. Then he says, "Very strong!" Then he turns and goes back to the table. The goblin pulls out some food from a small satchel under the table. He says, “None for you!” then he begins eating.

I realize that I’m in a desperate situation. I mutters to myself, *I’m ready to wake up from the nightmare now!* I even pinch myself. But this does not change my situation. I walk over to a corner of the room and sit down. I watch the goblin jailer finish his meal. The jailer’s eyes begin slowly closing. In moments, the jailer is snoring loudly.

I remember the lessons that Merval has taught me. Up until now I have chosen to not exercise my newfound powers, as meager as they are. I don’t want to let on that I’m being trained in the magical arts.

It’s dark in this dungeon and the jailer is fast asleep. I decides to focus my mind on the bars of the cell. Maybe I can use my mental energy to bend the bars just enough for me to pull my body through them. But that’s only the first step in escaping. I will still need to figure out how to slip out of a well-guarded castle. I will need weapons. I notice several mounted on the wall of the cavern near the sleeping jailer. I will have to get to those before the jailer awakens!

One thing I'm sure of is that I don't want to be in this cell when Lord Malvus comes to interrogate me. I'm sure that it will be far worse than our first encounter. I almost lost my mind that time. My only real hope is if Emilia and Grimalkin become aware of my absence and come to rescue me. I resolve to focus my mental energy on those cell bars!

Merval

Merval has made his way up the winding stairs to Merlin's chamber at the top of the center tower of the White Castle. He walks over to the door and begins to meow loudly. After five minutes of meowing, he hears Merlin's voice say, "Merval, I know that it's you at the door. Go away! I don't want to be bothered right now!"

Ordinarily, Merval would just leave at this point. But this is not an ordinary occasion. Merval must connect with Merlin and gain his assistance to free Robert. So, Merval changes tactics.

Merval transforms himself into a large gray panther. Instead of a cat's meow, Merval emits a loud screeching sound. He also begins to claw at the door. Merlin reacts immediately. He says, "Merval, I know what you are up to, but it won't work. I said that I want to be left alone right now!" Merval continues to screech and claw at the door.

Finally, Merlin relents. He says, "Ok, I will let you in, but this better be important!" The door opens. Merlin is standing there facing a huge gray panther. He says, "Merval, you made your point! So please transform back into a cat body again. Your panther persona is making me nervous!"

Merval's panther body begins the transformation. In a few seconds he's back in his cat body. Merval walks into Merlin's chamber. It's filled with shelves full of old dusty books, a collection of staffs and wands and a clothing rack filled with an assortment of cloaks, robes. and wizard's hats. In the center of the room is a pedestal. On the pedestal sits Merlin's crystal ball.

Merval is about to speak when Merlin interrupts him. He says, "Merval, I already know why you are here. The crystal ball tells me much about what is transpiring in this castle and throughout our world. Your human apprentice, Robert, has been abducted by the dark Lord Malvus. Lord Malvus has Robert imprisoned in a cell in his dungeon. You have come to enlist my help in freeing him."

Merval replies, "Master, that's indeed why I'm here. We could simply try and free him by force, but that would be what Lord Malvus would like us to do. His castle is well protected by goblins and gargoyles. Formidable weapons are mounted on the castle walls. Our losses would be heavy."

Merlin replies, "So, why should I help free Robert? Is he not the one selected by Grimalkin to be my eventual successor as sorcerer for the White Castle? Are you so eager to get rid of me?"

Merval replies, "Master, we don't intend to replace you, however, Robert is young and has the potential to develop his powers. Lord Malvus is growing stronger by the day. We must also strengthen ourselves to prevent him from retaking the White Castle and the portals to the human world and others." If Robert can be trained to become a sorcerer, he'll only enhance our strength in this world! We need you now more than ever! You must consider what is good for all of us, not just yourself! Remember that you were once a human, just like Robert. You were brought to the castle and trained by your master, Umberto before he passed. Later, you entered a portal to the human world where you performed great deeds. It's time for you to help train another, just as you were once trained, long ago."

Merlin ponders what Merval has said. He replies, "Merval, your words are wise. I have become old and selfish. I have disengaged from my responsibilities and hid in this tower too long. I will help you and Grimalkin to free Robert. I must first consult the crystal ball. Then I will descend to the throne room and meet with you all. In the meantime, summon Grimalkin, Emilia, the dragons, and felines. We will need all of them for my plan to work.

Merval says, “Thank you master. It’s good to have you back with us.” Merlin says, “It’s good to be back!”

Merval departs the room and climbs down the staircase. He enters the throne room and is greeted by Grimalkin and Emilia. He says, “Merlin will help us. Emilia, he wants you to summon the dragons.”

Merlin is in his chamber, gazing into his crystal ball. A cloud begins swirling inside it. He voices an incantation. The cloud begins to clear. In the center of the ball is the image of the Dark Castle. It’s a view made from the perspective of a particular eagle hovering over the castle. Merlin continues voicing incantations. The eagle begins a series of descending circles until resting its feet on a stone atop the castle wall.

The movements of the eagle have revealed the Dark Castles defenses to Merlin. While on the wall, the eagle has also surveyed the strength, location and movements of goblins camped inside and around the Dark Castle’s grounds. The eagle eyes a small mouse running across the interior base of the castle wall. Merlin voices yet another incantation.

Now the crystal ball is revealing the inside of the castle from the visual perspective of the mouse. The mouse slips under the door of the central structure. It makes its way down the spiral staircase and then to the dungeon below. The mouse quietly walks past the sleeping goblin. It, peers into each cage in the dungeon until it reaches the one where Robert is held. Once there, it stops and looks at Robert. Slowly it approaches him.

Robert

I have been focusing my mental energy on the bars of the cell. Thus far, I have achieved little progress in bending them. I'm beginning to feel a bit depressed. Then I notice a mouse slowly approaching me. This seems quite curious because mice will instinctively run from a human. But this mouse continues to approach me. When the mouse is just in front of me, it stands up on its hind legs and begins moving its mouth as if It's speaking with me. The mouses eyes lock onto mine.

I now understand. My friends in the White Castle have located me via this mouse. They will come soon to rescue me. This lifts my spirits. I mouth the words, "Thank you." The mouse gets back on all fours and slowly departs my cage. With renewed vigor, I resume focusing my mental energy on bending the cell bars.

Merlin

Merlin exits his chambers and descends the tower stairs. When he enters the throne room, he finds Grimalkin, Emilia, Merval and a host of cats and dragons in their human form. Merlin announces, "Robert is being held captive in a cage in the dungeon of Lord Malvus's Dark Castle. He's also aware that we know where he is.

Emilia asks, "Merlin, how do you propose that we rescue Robert?" Merlin replies, "I have a plan!" Then he looks around at everyone and asks, "What is the most powerful portal medium in the White Castle?" Grimalkin replies, "It's Gertrude's ring. The ring is stored in an ancient chest. The chest has not been opened in over one hundred years! I don't know if anyone here has the knowledge to use the ring."

Without hesitation, Merlin commands, "Bring the chest to me now!"

In a few minutes, Maisie and Sophie drag an old dusty chest into the throne room. They try and open it, but It's locked. Merlin says, "Step aside!" Then he pulls out a wand and waves it over the chest. He voices an incantation and places the wand on top of the chest. The wand begins glowing. Then it slowly starts changing shape until it morphs into the shape of a key. Merlin reaches for the key, picks it up and inserts it into the lock of the chest. There is an audible click. Merlin lifts the lid of the chest and reaches inside. He pulls out a ring. Merlin holds the ring up and studies it. The ring is made of white gold. At its center is a tiny red gemstone. Merlin slips the ring onto his finger. The gemstone immediately begins glowing. This brings a contented look to Merlin's face.

Merlin explains, "I gave this ring to Gertrude two centuries ago. It was a gift of great power. Gertrude was a great sorceress in her time. She was also my dear love. Gertrude has long since passed away. I had forgotten about the ring until Grimalkin mentioned it just a few minutes ago. Then I recalled that it was in Gertrude's chest. The ring has great power. Not even Lord Malvus knows about its existence. This ring can act as a portal. The red gemstone at its center has a unique quality. It allows the bearer of the ring to create a portal that's coupled with other portals bearing the same type of red gemstone. You see, long ago there was once one great red gemstone which had magical powers. The gemstone was cut into smaller stones by skilled elvish artisans. These stones were mounted on various objects which then had the power of portal creation. The greatest of these was Gertrude's ring.

Next, Merlin reaches into the chest and pulls out a two-foot-long tubular shaped rod. He holds it in his hands and utters an incantation. The rod begins to glow. Merlin strikes one end of the rod into the ground. It immediately transforms into a staff. Merlin comments, "This was another of my gifts to my dear Gertrude.

Merlin is standing before us with his ring in one hand and the glowing staff in the other.
He says, "I think that we now have all the tools that we need to rescue young Robert from the Dark Castle. Gather closely and I will tell all of you of my plan!"

The Dark Castle

Lakees comes running into the main structure of the castle. Then he runs down the hallway to Lord Malvus's chambers and begins pounding on the door with his fist. He cries out, "Lord Malvus, he's here approaching the main gate!" Lord Mavus replies, "Lakees! Is that you pounding on my door? I told you never to disturb me when I'm in my chamber! There better be a good reason for this intrusion! Who, is it that's approaching the gate?"

Lakees replies, "It's him! The sorcerer Merlin! He's at the main gate of the castle. He's just standing there! Should I have the guards confront him?"

Lord Malvus opens the door. He has an angry annoyed look on his face. He asks, "How do you know it's Merlin? And how did he get past your gargoyle patrols?"

Lakees replies, "I don't know how he got here! The patrols never saw him coming. He just suddenly appeared at the gate carrying a staff in his hand. It can only be Merlin. He's an old human in white robes. No one else in our world matches that description."

Lord Malvus says, “Did anyone ask Merlin what he wants?”

Lakees replies, “The guards did ask him. Merlin demanded to speak to you about your captive, Robert.”

Lord Malvus angrily yells, “You should have told me that in the first place!” Then he says, “Lakees, just in case It’s Merlin, have the goblins assemble by the gate and the gargoyles along the rooftops ready to attack Merlin on my command! Go now and carry out my instructions. I will keep Merlin busy until everyone is in position.”

Several minutes later, Lord Malvus emerges from his chamber wearing his black cloak. He walks down the hallway to the courtyard. From there he climbs up a stairway to the top of the wall just above the main gate. He sees a lone figure standing in front of the gate. There is no question. This is Merlin. The last time Lord Malvus saw Merlin was just after Lord Malvus was driven from the White Castle. It was a very long time ago, but he never forgot the sight of Merlin standing on the wall of the White Castle looking down at him as he retreated with what was left of his goblin and gargoyle army. That day, Lord

Malvus swore to take revenge on Merlin for bringing such humiliation upon him.

Now the tide has turned. Lord Malvus is standing on the wall of the Dark Castle looking at the ancient solitary figure of Merlin standing before the gate. His first urge is to order his guards to strike Merlin down, however, his curiosity is peaked. He's wondering what Merlin is doing here. Lord Malvus decides to wait a bit longer to exact his revenge on Merlin. He must satisfy his curiosity first.

Lord Malvus calls out, "Merlin, it's been so long since we last saw each other. What brings you to the gate of my Dark Castle?"

Merlin replies, "I assure you that this is not a social visit. I'm here to secure the release of young Robert. I know that you are holding him in a cell in your dungeon."

Lord Malvus replies, "What you say is true. I'm holding Robert in my dungeon. But why should I release him? Especially to you!"

"Because I have something you value to exchange for Robert."

"And what might that something be?"

"Me."

"That's an interesting trade. But I already have you. You are standing in front of my gate. I only need to order my guards to take you!"

"It would not be so easy to take me!" Merlin strikes the ground with his staff. A bolt of lightning shoots out the end of it and strikes the castle wall." A small section of stone dislodges and crumbles to the ground.

Lord Malvus replies, "An impressive display of power. It would take many of my guards to subdue you. But you are one and we are many!"

Merlin says, "I will lay down my staff as soon as Robert is allowed to pass out the gate."

Lord Malvus says, "Why would you sacrifice yourself for a human with no magical powers? What is he to you?"

"Robert is my apprentice. He's also to be my successor. He has just begun his training. I'm powerful, but old. Robert is young. I'm trading one life for another."

Lord Malvus quietly signals his guards. There is a large contingent hidden just behind the wall near the gate. A large number of gargoyles are also at the ready to attack Merlin from above. Malvus's plan is to have them rush Merlin just after the gate opens and he steps inside.

Lord Malvus says, "Merlin, your offer has some appeal to me. Would you be willing to enter the castle. We can meet to discuss it further."

Merlin replies, "Yes, I would be willing to do that."

Lord Malvus nods to the goblins manning the mechanism that opens the gate doors. The goblins begin turning a large wheel that drives a series of large gears. Merlin sees that the doors are opening, so he begins to walk forward. As he passes through the now fully open gate, goblins come rushing at him from both sides. Merlin has been anticipating this move. He waves his staff in a circular motion above his head. This unleashes a powerful bolt of energy that strikes the first wave of attacking goblins.

They're sent reeling backwards. A second wave attacks of goblins attacks.

Lord Malvus signals Lakees who has been waiting at the top of the wall with a large contingent of gargoyles. They fly off the wall to attack Merlin. But before any of the attackers can reach him, the red gemstone on Merlin's ring begins to glow. Immediately a large black portal opens in the center of the courtyard. Dragons and panthers come leaping through the portal and charge the goblins and gargoyles. In moments, the entire courtyard has become a battlefield with dragons and panthers tearing the overmatched goblins and gargoyles to pieces. The courtyard is awash in green goblin blood. The goblins manning the giant crossbows on the castle walls are attempting to turn then around so that they can be aimed at the dragons fighting in the courtyard. Emilia, Maisie, and Sophie fly up the walls and set the crossbows ablaze with their dragon breath. All of the crossbows are burning as are the goblins that were manning them.

Lord Malvus aims his wand at the dragons. A bolt of magical energy leaps off the tip of the wand and strikes Sophie. Sophie immediately tumbles to the ground.

Merlin sees this and aims his staff in the direction of Lord Malvus. Malvus counters by aiming his wand and directing a stream of energy at Merlin. The beams lock into each other. For a few moments the beams struggle back and forth. Merlin increases his focus. The beam from his staff continues to consume the beam from Lord Malvus's wand. Eventually, Merlin's beam contacts Malvus's wand which is incinerated. Malvus is thrown backwards to the floor of the wall. He gets up and ducts below the battlement as Merlin continues to direct his energy beam from his staff in his direction. This begins to chip away at the battlement shielding Lord Malvus. Lakees is hiding next to him.

Lord Malvus is shocked at the turn of events. How could this have happened? What trick of sorcery did Merlin play to allow the dragons and panthers to magically materialize inside his castle. He grabs ahold of Lakees and says, "We must go to my quarters and grab the crystal ball. It cannot fall into the hands of Merlin! Then we will go to the dungeon and seize Robert. Robert is the only bargaining chip we can use against Merlin and his minions. Lord Malvus, Lakees and a dozen goblins climb down the wall stairs and run into the main building. They secure the doors behind them with a thick wooden beam. Having secured the door, Malvus retrieves his crystal ball and then proceeds down the circular stairway towards the dungeon.

The Dungeon

I have succeeded in weakening the cell bars just enough that I can separate them and slip through. The sound wakes the goblin guard from his sleep. But It's too late. I grab the guards rod and rap him over the head with it. The guard crashes to the floor. Then I hear many footsteps approaching. I notice an axe and sword that are mounted on the wall. I grab both of them and retreat deeper into the dungeon. I want to find a place where I can hide, but also view my pursuers.

Emilia has noticed that Lord Malvus, Lakees and a dozen goblins have run into the main building and slammed the door shut. She's still in her dragon body, so she flies down to the courtyard and stands in front of the door. She lets out a breath of fire. The fire incinerates the door. It caves inwards. Emilia realizes that her dragon body will not fit in the hallway, so she reverts to her human warrior body. Emilia draws her sword and runs into the building and down the circular staircase leading to the dungeon. She's closely followed by Grimalkin and Merval, who are in still their fierce panther bodies.

Lord Malvus has reached the dungeon and sees the guard lying on the floor with green blood oozing from a head wound. He looks at my locked cell. There is no one inside, but Malvus notices the bent bars. Malvus yells, "He escaped! Find him now!" Immediately Lakees and the goblins fan out and begin searching all of the cells in the dungeon. Meanwhile, I have been watching from a dark corner at the back of the dungeon. I realizes that there are too many goblins for me to overpower them all. I can only hope for help to arrive soon.

Just then I'm spotted. A goblin points at me and says, "Lord Malvus. He's over there!" The goblins immediately cease searching and walk in the direction that the goblin is pointing. I realize that I must come out now and fight for my life. I emerge from my hiding place. I'm swinging my axe in one hand and a sword in the other. Lord Malvus is standing behind the goblins and yelling, "Get him! But he must be alive! He does me no good dead!"

I feint an attack at the goblins. They, back away briefly. Then they close in on me once more. The nearest goblin attempts to strike me with a club. I sidestep his attack and counters with my axe. It lodges in the breastbone of the goblin. The goblin lets out a scream. Green blood is spurting out of his wound. A second goblin steps forward and swings his axe at me. I deflects the blow with my sword but fall backwards on the ground. The goblin swings his axe downward at me. I roll to the side to avoid it. The axe just misses me. I thrust my sword upwards into his throat. The goblin make a gurgling sound and then collapses next to me.

Just then Emilia and the panthers burst into the dungeon. They charge at the goblins who are attacking me. The goblins turn around and panic at the sight of the charging panthers. Emilia swings her sword and lops off the head of the nearest goblin. Then she swings it again and chops off another goblin's arm. She's moving at lightning speed, cutting through the goblins as if they were butter. The panthers have each jumped on top of goblins and ripped out their throats. Green blood is splattered everywhere.

I have used the distraction to regain my feet. Then I enter the fray, hacking at the panicking goblins with my sword. I'm energized! I'm also wondering if this is what Sir Lancelot felt like when he was in battle!

Lord Malvus has been quietly backing away from the fight. He realizes that the cause is lost and if he remains, he'll meet the same fate as the goblins. He no longer has his wand, but he has his crystal ball tucked under his cloak. He and Lakees retreat out of the dungeon through a secret door. When all of the goblins have been killed, Emilia look around and says, "Where is Lord Malvus?" We search around the dungeon but cannot find him. Grimalkin has reverted to her cat body. She begins sniffing around. She finds a strange looking rock in the wall. There is a fine line tracing in the shape of a doorway. I push on it with my hand. The door suddenly begins sliding open. It exposes a narrow passageway. Merval says, "Lord Malvus has escaped through this doorway!"

Emilia says, "There is no point in chasing Lord Malvus now. One could easily get lost in a maze of underground caves."

So, we leave the dungeon and return to the courtyard. The battle is over now. Any surviving goblins have fled out the gate. Most of the gargoyles flew away soon after the dragons and panthers appeared. They wanted no part of being set fire by dragon's breath. Goblin bodies are strewn everywhere around the courtyard.

Sophie is lying on the ground. She has a wound on her right wing from the energy beam that Lord

Malvus has struck her with. Merval and Gimalkin are attending to her and directing a magic curing spell towards her wound. Soon Sophie regains her feet but will likely not be able to fly for the next few days until fully healed.

Merlin walks into the center of the yard. He looks at me and says, “Robert, it’s good to see you are in one piece. Your capture served as a catalyst for the expulsion of Lord Malvus from the Dark Castle. It also jarred me out of my stubbornness.

Emilia says, “Today, Robert proved himself worthy of joining us. He orchestrated his own escape from a cell in the dungeon, overcame the goblin guard and acquitted himself well in battle against a large number of goblins.”

Merlin says, “Robert, it will be my privilege to oversee your training. There is much knowledge that I can pass on to you and perhaps not a lot of time to do it. I suggest we return to the White Castle and continue your training as soon as possible. Meanwhile, we need to organize a contingent of felines and dragons to ensure that Lord Malvus does not try and sneak back into the Dark Castle. A search of the castle is in order. We need to find Lord Malvus’s crystal ball and any other powerful artifacts he kept in the Dark Castle." Merval responds, "I have already searched Lord Malvus's chamber. I found the pedestal, but the crystal ball is not there. I fear that Malvus has taken it with him when he fled."

Merlin replies, "That's most unfortunate. The crystal ball has great power and will allow Malvus to continue to be a menace in the future. We will have to remain vigilant. He has been somewhat defanged for now but will most certainly want to take back the Dark Castle and more when he has regained his strength.

Lord Malvus

Lord Malvus and Lakees have been walking through miles of underground tunnels and caverns. It has been a long time since Lord Malvus has been down here, but his crystal ball has become useful in insuring he does not lose his way. They reach an underground stream and follow it. Lord Malvus remembers that the stream leads to a rock face. At the rock face he and Lakees can climb up a rock staircase until they reach a cave that leads into the forest, several miles from the Dark Castle. From there they will walk towards the dark lands of the east. It's there where Lord Malvus's future will be cast.

Lord Malvus realizes that he made a terrible mistake by allowing Merlin to trick him into opening the gate and allowing him to come inside the Dark Castle. Malvus totally underestimated Merlin's power. How could he have been so foolish? Once inside the castle, Merlin opened a portal allowing the dragons and panthers to run amok and destroy his minions. Now Malvus and Lakees are alone. But Merlin did not get Malvus's crystal ball. With it, he'll rebuild his power in the dark lands. But this time, he must seek out even more powerful allies. The goblins were unreliable. The ones not killed by the dragons and felines ran away. The gargoyles flew away. They were all cowards!

But now, Lord Malvus realizes that he's no longer powerful enough to confront Merlin and his minions. There is only one course of action that he can take now. He must make the long journey to the Forbidden Mountains. Then he must find the hidden secret cave deep below. It will be an arduous journey, but it must be done.

Once inside the cave he'll travel along a narrow passage deeper and deeper under the mountains until he reaches the inner sanctum of his old master, Azal. Malvus had studied the black magic arts under Azal for many years. Malvus grew ever more powerful under Azal's tutelage.

Azal had passed much of his knowledge to Malvus. He decided that Malvus, was ready to become his instrument of conquest. Azal told Malvus to leave and not return until the White Castle and the portals were taken. When Malvus succeeded in that task Azal proclaimed him the lord of the White Castle. He then instructed Malvus to use the portals to enter and conquer the world of humans.

Initially, Lord Malvus was successful, but in time, the forces of good prevailed and Malvus was driven back. He retreated to the Dark Castle. But now, he has lost even that!

Lord Malvus knows that Master Azal will be angry to see him return as a failure. But Malvus has nowhere else to go. He must throw himself down at Azal's feet and beg forgiveness for his failures. It will be a great humiliation, but It's his only chance to recharge his power. Of course, Azal could choose to cast him aside. It's a risk that Malvus is prepared to take.

After hours of navigating the underground passages, Lord Malvus enters the cavern that he has been seeking. Upon a throne chair in the middle of the cavern sits his old master, Azal. Behind Azal flows a river of molten lava. The lava glows and provides a deep red lighting to the cavern.

Azal's appears is just as Malvus remembers him. His head is cloaked. But under the hood, he can see the scaley green skin and sunken, glowing red eyes. Azal is surrounded by smaller devilish looking creatures with red skin, tails and small, insect type wings. Each has a belt around its waist carrying a sheathed dagger. One devil runs up to Azal and whispers in his ear.

Azal turn towards Malvus and presents a stern look. A terrified Lakees hides behind Malvus. He's trying to bring as little attention to himself as possible.

Azal says, "Malvus, why have you come here. I told you to not return until you have conquered the White Castle and the world of the humans. My spies tell me that they have conquered you! You return to me as a disgrace and a failure!"

Malvus replies, "I had nowhere else to turn. I was deceived by that miserable sorcerer, Merlin. I did not have sufficient power to counter his magic. I have come to you asking for your help. I must get my revenge on Merlin, the dragons, and felines." Then he presents his crystal ball and places at Azal's feet as tribute.

Azal replies "I don't help failures. When I told you to not return until you succeeded, I meant it! You have failed me and will not get a second chance!" Azal glares at Malvus with his eyes. A stream of red energy shoots out of his eyes and envelops Malvus. Malvus lets out a terrifying cry. His body contorts inside an envelope of red crackling energy. It rises off the ground. Malvus is still crying out in pain. Azal directs his body through the air and into the hot flowing lava. For a moment his body floats on the lava but then is drawn within it. Malvus is no more. Then he says, “Oh, I forgot to say, thank you for the gift!” Azal signals for one of his devils to pick up the crystal ball and place it on the table next to him.

Azal turns towards Lakees who is cowering. He says, “So what will I do with you my winged friend?” Lakees replies in a trembling voice, “Most powerful one. Don’t kill me. I only wish to serve. I will do whatever you command.” Azal says, “I see that you have a large set of wings. I have always wanted to wear wings. You may be of use to me yet!”

Once again, Azal’s eyes lock onto Lakees. Lakees’s body is enveloped in crackling red energy. He’s crying out in pain. But instead of casting Lakees into the lava flow, Azal pulls him into his own body. Soon Lakees disappears and all that’s left is Azal standing before his throne chair. But now, Azal has a large pair of wings attached to his own back. He begins flapping his wings and slowly rises off the floor. Azal flies around the cavern a few times before setting his feet back on the ground. He says, "Thank you Lakees!"

Azal addresses the red devil creatures surrounding him, "These wings will take some getting used to, but I think they will serve me well when confronting the dragons. My mistake was sending a boy to do a man's job. Now it will be I who conquers the White Castle and the world of humans! There is much work to do. I will raise an army like none this word has ever seen. Then we will take back the Dark Castle and strike the White Castle!"

Three Months Later

It's a beautiful summer afternoon in Mountain View. I'm sitting on a chaise lounge chair by my pool. Emilia is similarly seated with Grimalkin in her lap. A lot has happened since I was freed from the dungeon in the Dark Castle many months ago. Merlin and Merval have been training me in the magical arts. My powers have grown considerably. I can even communicate telepathically with the dragons and felines. I can read minds too. It's strange being able to eavesdrop into the thoughts of others.

Emilia cautioned me that reading human's minds should only be done if there is a good reason to do it. Otherwise, it'd best to leave the thoughts of other humans to themselves. An unsuspecting person can freak out if they suddenly sense a foreign presence inside of their head. So, I limit my telepathic communications with other telepathic entities like the dragons, felines and of course, Merlin.

One of my newfound powers is that I have learned how to use my bedframe as a portal while I'm awake. This is allowing me to move freely between my human world and the magical world of the White Castle. I no longer travel there in my dreams. Dreams have become reality for me!

I have asked Merlin if I will have the power to change my form to that of a dragon or other living entity like Emilia is able to do. Merlin explains that even he cannot directly change form. But he says that he'll teach me how to be a warg. A warg is a person who can enter the mind of a creature and perceive the world through that creature's senses. The warg can even control the creature's actions.

Merlin explains that he was able to locate my cell in the Dark Castle by first warging into the mind of an eagle that he sent to spy on the Dark Castle. Then he warged into the mind of a mouse who was near to the eagle when it landed on the castle wall. Once in control of the mouse, Merlin directed it to enter the dungeon and locate me in my cell. I reply, "So that's how you did that. I thought it was an enchanted mouse that found me." Merlin replies, "It was actually me inside the mouse's mind."

I realize that there is a lot to learn if I'm to become anywhere near as good of a sorcerer as Merlin. Emilia and Merval seem to think that I have been making great progress in my training. I can project a magical energy beam with or without a wand in my hand. I still find the wand as a more accurate and powerful instrument for projecting energy beams. It helps me to focus better when I have an object in my hand. Besides, that's how Harry Potter did it in the books and movies!

Emilia was impressed enough with my sword and axe fighting skills that she gave me my own set of white chain mail armor. It even has the dragon insignia emblazoned on it!

An opportunity came to wear it in battle when a group of goblin bandits began terrorizing and robbing dwarfs and elves who were travelling along one of the trails in a nearby forest. The problem got out of hand when one party of elves was found dead along the trail.

Emilia took on human form as did Maisie, Sophie, and Lola. We disguised ourselves as elf merchants and rode a wagon along the very forest trail that the goblin bandits were terrorizing. We were all wearing armor and weapons hidden under cloaks of a style typically worn by travelers. The cart was pulled by two work horses. We made sure that sacks, presumably filled with goods were visible on the wagon. This would surely attract bandits.

We came across a felled tree that blocked our passage on the trail. In moments we were surrounded by two dozen large, fearsome looking goblins.

The goblin leader demanded that we turn over our wagon and horses or else they would kill us all. I put on a ruse, begging the goblin leader to let us pass. I said, “The wagon contains our goods to be sold at the main market in the White Castle. If you take it, we have nothing left! Please have mercy on us. We can give you a portion of what we have, but please don’t take all of it!”

As expected, the goblin leader laughed and then said, “I gave you a chance to escape with your lives. You did not take it. You will now pay the price!” He nodded to his fellow bandits. The goblins immediately drew their swords, clubs, and axes. They approached the wagon from all sides. We cringed and feigned terror as they approached us. The goblins were laughing. They assumed we would not resist in any way. When the goblins were almost upon us, we threw off our cloaks and drew our swords. The goblins were taken by surprise. Initially they fought, but they were no match for the five of us.

I leapt off of the wagon and began swinging my sword at the nearest goblin. The sharp blade of my sword found the goblin's neck. The head flew off of the goblin's body. Green blood was spurting everywhere. Emilia and the others moved with lightning speed. Out of the corner of my eye, I could see them parrying the goblin's attacks and striking back with deadly accuracy. Within a few minutes, half of the goblins were lying on the ground bleeding spewing green blood. The others ran into the woods. This included the goblin leader of the bandits. He wanted no part of us. Needless to say, there was no longer any trouble for travelers along that trail.

So here we are relaxing by the pool. For now, with Lord Malvus defeated, peace has returned to the magical lands of the White Castle. But peace never lasts for long, I wonder what challenges may lie ahead for us!

Merlin

Merlin and Merval are walking up the circular stairway to Merlin's tower chamber. Merlin says, "Merval, I have something to show you." They enter Merlin's chambers and walk over to the crystal ball.

Merlin removes the cloth cover revealing a clear cylinder sitting on a pedestal. They both peer into the crystal ball. Merlin places his hands over the ball and issues an incantation. The once clear ball begins to cloud up. At first the clouds are a clear white color, then they begin to turn dark.

Merlin says, "Merval, after Lord Malvus was expelled from the Dark Castle, the dark clouds covering the east had receded. The birds and land creatures had returned to the forest of the eastern lands. This was a sign that evil had receded from many of the lands in our world."

Merlin continues, "Recently, I the crystal ball has revealed dark clouds gathering in the east once more. I fear that something foul is afoot there. An evil presence has returned to our world. Even worse, Its spreading fast. At first, I thought that Lord Malvus may be rallying his scattered minions, however, It's too soon for that to have happened. We dealt him a severe blow when we captured the Dark Castle and scattered his minions."

Merlin continues saying, "I believe that another evil force is rising, and It's doing so very quickly. We must warn the dragons and felines that have been guarding the Dark Castle. They must be prepared for the worst. I will dispatch several eagles to the dark eastern lands. Perhaps they can uncover the presence behind the spreading evil. Also, summon Grimalkin, Emilia, and Robert. We will surely need them if we are to combat this growing evil.

"Our work is never done!"

A Note to Readers

I grew up in a suburb of New York City. My family owned a large Tudor home similar to the house that the main character in my story grew up in.

The mansion in Mountain View, California is an actual place where I rented a room soon after I came out to California in the late 1970's. I had just started a job as an engineer at Intel Corporation and an acquaintance told me that a room was available for rent in this house. The mansion is just as described in the story. It was a speakeasy during prohibition. It had numerous antiques inside. The basement is as I described it. I attended several parties there.

The attic of the mansion was borrowed from my childhood home in New York. Many of the objects I discovered in the attic as a child are described in the story. Of course, there was no magical bedframe. That was my own creation.

The town of Capitola is one of my favorite places to visit on the coast of California. Capitola is exactly as I have described it. I have enjoyed many a sunny afternoon boogie boarding, swimming and occasionally surfing there.

Castro Street in Mountain View is as described. I spent many afternoons and evenings walking down this street, shopping and then eating at one of its' many restaurants.

I find cats fascinating and mysterious. I often wonder what they know that I don't. You will find that many of my books have cats as central characters.

I dream almost every night. My dreams tend to be quite vivid. Again, several of my books are centered around dreams.

I have enjoyed reading book series like J. R. R. Tolkien's Lord of the Rings, and George R. R. Martin's A Song of Ice and Fire. I named the principal dragon in my story after Emilia Clarke, the actress who played Daenerys Targaryen in the Game of Thrones TV series. Other dragons were named after actresses Maisie Williams and Sophie Turner from Game of Thrones.

Arbak Gaming is not a real company but is representative of the many startup companies that have flourished in the Santa Clara Valley in recent decades. I spent several years at one such startup company. Sadly, it was not as successful as Arbak Gaming.

I combined all of the above elements into The Cat, The Dragon, and Me.

If you enjoyed the book, please write a review and/or leave a rating.

Readers may also enjoy my four-book fantasy medieval series beginning with **Abri's Quest**. I also have a short story collection titled **Twisted Fantasy Stories**. For cat lovers, you may like my Sci-Fi series beginning with **Galaxy Cat**. My book, **Dreamer,** also has a cat as a principal character.

Thank you,

Barwell Hollings

Printed in Great Britain
by Amazon

37047562R00089